WHAT'S SO FUNNY

A NOVEL BY JOSEPH TORRA

WHAT'S SO FUNNY

PRESSED WAFER | BOSTON

PRESSED WAFER

9 COLUMBUS SQUARE, BOSTON, MASSACHUSETTS 02116

WHEN I got home from my teeth cleaning and looked in the bathroom mirror, I discovered a green crust clinging inside my upper right nostril. A half an hour earlier I'd stared up at Mildred wearing her baggy blue medical uniform and clunky white shoes. Looking down from behind her clear plastic mask, she poked and scraped; periodically she sat up, raised her mask like a welder, and fidgeted with gadgets. Sit up and rinse, she said. I sat up and rinsed. Then she pulled down her mask, returned to work to sounds of piped-in soft rock, and every few minutes asked something like, Will it rain today? NNNNNG, I answered with my jaw wide open and both her hands in my mouth. I fantasized about having sex with Mildred right there, even though she looks like Olive Oyl on steroids. Something about being that close, her hands in my mouth, and when I saw her face behind the mask, her dull complexion and unremarkable brown eyes, I would. Maybe she thought the same about me. Maybe it happens to her a lot with her hands forever in people's mouths, so close she sees every imperfection.

As I imagined Mildred mounting me on the dentist chair, she was eyeing my snot. Imagine how it must have looked from her angle, with those lights shining up my cave so close and personal? If I had her email address I could apologize, promise never again to come and get my teeth cleaned without first checking for snots. I could call the office but that would mean having to speak with her. There could never be anything between us now.

FRIDAY NIGHT I'll use old stuff. Familiar stuff. Ethnic standards. Why not? The bit about my Aunt Josie dying at my cousin Lucy's wedding gets them every time. And it's true. She keeled over face down in her macaroni. By the time they wheeled her out in a stretcher, the macaroni was cold and nobody wanted to eat. Uncle Vinny, Lucy's father and Josie's sister, stood up and yelled so loud the room shook, ok now everyone eat your dinner and drink some wine! Until he died he hated his sister Josie for ruining his daughter's wedding. Wherever she is now, he always said, she owes me twenty thousand. I'll work some of the gambling stuff in. My old man and his goombah friends, how I knew my father had been gambling too much when we ate spaghetti with garlic and olive oil, because that's what my mother could afford. My father used to say that people he knew, usually his deceased father or his dead sister, came to him in

6

dreams and told him to play a certain number or daily double. I liked spaghetti with garlic and olive oil I didn't mind. So my grandfather or dead aunt would appear in my father's dreams and say, hey Gianni, tomorrow call the bookie and tell him play a certain number. I'll work in the list of my Italian girl-friends. Most of them weren't my girlfriends but girls I knew. And how my first love Tina Zamboni would only do oral sex because she was saving it for her marriage. If the guys are out in numbers, I'll throw in the part about how she could suck the chrome off a bumper.

I STUCK WITH my plan. It went over like flat beer. Over time there are fewer and fewer Italian-Americans around, or maybe they're too much like the woodwork now so the younger folks don't get the cultural references. They want the gangster stuff. All they know is *The Sopranos*. My generation it was *The Godfather*. When you're Italian you always get the Mafia comments. Everybody thinks you're con-nected. It'll take a WOP president to change it. One thing for sure, the White House will serve better food than any other administration.

I should have finished with the Saint Tina of the Virgin Blowjob line, but used the chrome and bum-per routine instead. That drew snarls from a group of women gathered around a table to my left. One of them snapped back, I couldn't hear exactly what she said because of the snarling, something about the size of my bumper. They were there to see the lesbian who as it turned out, had several funny moments and besides, she was cute. That's part of another bit of mine about gender and sex and how some guys love lesbians. I stared at the woman in the audience who had interrupted me, pissed that she'd blown my punch line and the ending of my show. Blame the church I said angrily. I don't know why.

The third comedian came from a small country in North Africa who did a bit about sneaking out of his country to get to America, and paying people to take him across the desert, and how he nearly starved and was forced to drink camel piss. He had lots of stuff about camel dicks and camel balls and guys wanting to fuck him up the ass at an oasis. He spoke with a heavy accent that made it hard to understand him, but he had a catch phrase: every day to pray, get to U.S.A.

THE PROBLEM WITH working new material into an older bit means I have to remove some material already in the bit to make room. Yesterday an Italian airline pilot was convicted of manslaughter. He was piloting a plane off the coast of Sicily when mechanical problems made it apparent that the plane would crash. Instead of going into emergency mode, the pilot first prayed. His delayed reaction, the court ruled, was partially responsible for the 14 lost lives. The pilot argued that there were 28 people on the plane. God, he said, had intended to kill everyone that day but when he heard the pilot's prayers, he showed mercy and cut the number of deaths in half.

Recently I worked in stuff about the right-to-lifer who shot a doctor who was pro-abortion while the doctor was attending church. I haven't got it right, I could remove it and replace it with the Italian pilot material. People get queasy when you attempt a laugh at a dead fetus, or dead doctor, or dead enemy soldier, and whether or not God has priorities and if so, is he tending to them?

I knew there was no God the moment I learned there was no Santa Claus. If everyone would lie about Santa, they'd lie about God. My Uncle Vinny always said go to church just in case. I used to fart in church, while the organ played, and the chorus, those creaky old fucks, sang out God's praises. I'd let them rip, and watched nearby churchgoers catch wind of my curdy psalms.

I PLANNED ON STOPPING for tacos after visiting my mother. There's a joint in Lynn all the Latinos eat there. But I lost my appetite after what happened. When I got to the nursing home I could hear scream-ing as soon as the elevator door opened. That's not unusual in the home, but in this case I recognized the voice as my mother's. As I got closer her words became clearer. I'm going to be sick, she said, and I turned the corner just in time to see her vomit on the shiny floor. Oh my God, she screamed, she shit all over my room!

Apparently another patient had to take a crap and unable to locate her room wandered into my mother's room, sat on her chair and proceeded to shit herself silly. There she remained squirming in it until my mother walked in. We sat out on a sofa near the fish tanks. She talked at me. She thought I was one of the orderlies. She shit all over my room, she said, and it made me sick. I told her things would be fine now and every few minutes she would gag as if to puke again. It was awful, she said, it was all over the place. I had to continually reassure her that the room would be cleaned and disinfected as she said she wasn't going to go back and she wouldn't be able to forget how it looked and smelled and how the woman had smeared it all over herself. What was she doing with it, she wanted to know. I hadn't an answer. We went down to the first floor, sat on a sofa by the fish tanks there. She was beginning to recognize me, but had no idea that I'd been upstairs and knew what happened. She shit all over the place, she said and told over again about how she rubbed herself with it. Then at lunchtime I brought her to the dining room and left her at her seat talking at the woman sitting across from her at the table. I drove right past the taco joint on my way home.

My Uncle Vinny used to say a lot of things. Never take a baloney sandwich to a banquet. If God wanted to waste a brain he would give it to an Irishman not a woman. Never watch the colored television shows, you boost the ratings. Colored women don't wear underwear. I was five or six at the time. What kind of thing is this to tell a five year old? I found it hard to believe that colored women didn't wear underwear. I asked him. Uncle Vinny why don't colored women wear underwear? Don't be a wise guy he responded. Uncle Vinny opted for early retirement. He worked construction and paid a guy to hit him on the head with a shovel. I've known some stupid people in my life and my Uncle Vinny was one.

Then there was Victor Marino, a teenaged friend who spent his time lifting weights or placing his mattress up against the bedroom wall then punching it. He flunked out of vocational school and worked for a moving company. He couldn't read a menu. Later he got married and when he had free time he punched his wife. Someone shouts that's not funny. There are other rumblings. I say let me get to the punch line. There's nothing funny about a man punching his wife. Was that the waitress's voice? I've lost it now. It's no use. I attempt a transition to the stupid roofer who nailed his foot to the roof with a hi-tech nail gun. The nail went right through the bone, and they had to get him down by first cutting out the section of the roof his foot was nailed to. On the news he said he thanked God that nothing worse happened. They always say I thank God I didn't die or I thank God I won the lottery or I thank God our beagle Sam made it back alive after a three thousand mile trek across the wilderness as if God is up there deciding, ok let's see, today, you the roofer in Indiana, nail your right foot to the roof, you in New Hampshire, win the lottery, you lost beagle Sam, return home safely.

I don't know where I am. I somehow have my God stuff mixed up with my stupid material. It happens sometimes. The crowd, if you can call it that, doesn't seem to notice. They stopped paying attention since my bit about Victor Marino beating his wife. This is a rare moment I can say anything and nobody will notice.

Someone noticed. I asked, Would anyone like to come up and pop the puss-filled boil on my ass? Someone said, hey man what the fuck? Later as the place emptied, the waitress came up to me and said that it wasn't really her business, but several customers complained. They just didn't think you were funny, she reported. All the ass boils and puss. I told her I didn't think I was any worse than the guy who went on after me. She said he was the best one of the night. After all, it is entertainment, she added.

The young man in question had a shtick that he never slept. How he ended up not sleeping was this long convoluted story that had to do with a rare disease that caused him to wet himself any time he fell asleep. Awake everything worked fine but when he slept things flowed uncontrollably. He moved about slowly, did a lot of yawning, kept his eyes half-mast, though he could have been stoned, and wore pajamas and slippers. His speech was slow and quiet. Every so often he did a set-up with I'm so tired, and some people in the audience asked how tired are you? How long have you been doing this, the waitress wanted to know. I told her my story of being a kid and doing my impersonations of Fred Caposella calling the races at Hialeah. In Fred's voice I said, Thank you Tommy, and good afternoon racing fans. She said maybe you should do impersonations.

Last night I couldn't sleep. I took two over-the-counter sleep tabs. I tried reading. I tried masturbating. This can backfire if the stroking makes me sleepy but also brings on a piss and I have to get up. I tried a drink. I tried chanting my mantra over and over while lying on my back with my arms folded over my chest the way Jill taught me. I tried working on the new bit about the young Mormon men who work the streets. Clean-cut, upright fellows in their white shirts and ties, they look like IRS agents and stop you to talk about Joseph Smith and The Book of Mormon—some guy who claimed to have a revelation that was clearly some kind of psychotic delusion.

Last resort I turned on the television and began the cycle of surfing through the news, old comedy reruns, music and video channels, cooking shows, soft core porn where I stopped for a few moments to watch two skinny women with oversize fake breasts share a double-ended dildo, the religious stations, various movies, history and science shows, I passed the comedy station without stopping—it makes me too upset and angry to watch—and landed on one of the Duke's lesser-known westerns. Something wasn't right and I switched back to the comedy station. I felt sick to my stomach like I did the first time I saw the performance, and how awful the color of my shirt looked on screen—over twenty years and at least twenty pounds ago, that puke-yellow shirt, mullet to die for—black Chuck Taylors and black jeans. Lenny Marx hosts three rising comedians, one of the early cable things. My big break.

It was the bit about my mob cousin, who never worked a day in his life and claimed to sell magazines. The kind of thing I would never do today. The crowd likes it. Then I turn to the wife material. I was still married. Claire hated it when I used her in my

14

work. Comedians have to be shits I told her. Nothing is sacred. Most of the stuff I said wasn't even true. I had one about how my wife didn't like oral sex. Claire loved oral sex. In fact she preferred it. The good thing is, after we divorced, I could use the same material. My ex-wife hated oral sex sounds even better than my wife hates oral sex.

My Uncle Vinny used to say, a woman is good for two things: making babies and taking care of the house. I like smart women. Maybe not in short-term relationships, but if you're going to get on with someone for any length of time, you need someone who'll give you a run for your money at Scrabble. I learned to cook for myself. Claire couldn't cook. I can't find anyone to have sex with. People say of course you can find someone to have sex with. I say show me, prostitutes aside, no offense intended.

What's with cleavage? Why can't I go to my doctor's office without worrying that the breasts on the woman who checks me in aren't going to flop out unannounced on her clipboard? And then the nurse's titties are popping out and then the doctor's intern's featuring her set. Is it some kind of in-joke? Is the whole world fucking and sucking in one big sex orgy behind my back? And at the gigs, there they are, tits. The dark inviting allure of cleavage everywhere I look. I point some of them out. Do you mind if I put my microphone there while I take a sip of water? What's the proper etiquette? Are you supposed to look? Look away? If a woman is putting her breasts on display does that mean she wants them to be appreciated? And now you got all these women with implants. Me, I like the real thing. I know I know. A lot of guys say tits are tits.

My father told me some stupid things when I was a kid. I think most parents tell their kids stupid things. Santa Claus and God are the two biggies. The Easter Bunny? You've got to be kidding me—a bunny that hops around the world, and delivers baskets full of candy. And what about the tooth fairy? It's not fair because kids are gullible. They believe these things. They have no reason to doubt adults who appear so wise and worldly, reasonable and responsible.

I grew up in Medford, Massachusetts. People from Medford are known to pronounce it Meffa. But I went to college, and live one mile away, so I only say Meffa when I'm drunk, because when you're drunk you let your guard down and it's back to basics. In Medford there was a big hill near my house. On top of the hill stood a radio tower, painted red and white, with a blinking red light on top. I was five or six at the time, and I asked my father what the blinking light was for. It's a signal tower, he said. If the light stops blinking, it means we're going to be attacked. Attacked? Who would attack us, I asked?

The enemy, he said. If somebody's going to attack us the light will stop blinking.

I believed him. For days, maybe weeks or more, every chance I had I went to the window, or watched from our yard. I rushed home from school and what relief when I fixed my eyes on the tower, to see that light blinking. I don't know when or how, but eventually I learned the light served other purposes. Why would a full-grown adult tell a kid such a thing? Mind you, this was at the height of the cold war, when at school they were still making us drill, as if getting under your desk would save you when they drop the big one.

At least my father didn't believe in God. He never went to church if he did. He never talked about God if he did. I supposed the best advice he ever gave me was don't wear white sox with dress clothes, and if you want to make good meatballs mix some pork in with the beef. He wasn't stupid. He was pretty good at working out the races for the day. He was imaginative, and often came up with unusual configurations. My Uncle Vinny always said, what are you crazy, you think you're Houdini? Once in a great while his hunches paid off, and when they did, my father would hit big. At his funeral Uncle Vinny lamented that my father just hit the trifecta the day before he took the heart attack and died. My mother found the three grand in his wallet and used it to cater the funeral party. I remember the eggplant.

I'm FED UP with the Baby Boomers, the so-called Woodstock Generation and our endless, tiresome crap about peace and love. If I hear one more person of my generation spew a platitude about how songs in our time really had meaning, and people cared about things. You know who you are. You shop at Whole Foods. Everything is whole. And you complain about music the young kids listen to, and say you can't understand the lyrics—the same thing your parents said about your music.

And the guys, professional, lots of architects, slight paunch, bald on top what few gray strands left down below tied in a pony tail, earring, worrying about their 401(k)s. What happened? Where did those millions of people who were marching and thinking about the future go? The majority of them are responsible for voting-in Ronald Reagan. Get back to the land and get my soul free my ass. Get back to a big lot and house in the suburbs of a predominantly white community, and pay hundreds of bucks to see The Stones or The Eagles on their greatest hits tours. And the New Agers, star gazers, herbal-shakers, meditaters and yoga fakers, Buddha sayers and guru payers. They reject the charlatanry of their parents' religions for one of their own choosing. You know who you are. The difference between the priest and a Buddhist monk is the uniform.

It's not religion I hate. Well, maybe I do hate religion. It's not that I don't think people have the right

to believe what they want. It's that they want everyone else to believe what they believe. I'm an atheist.
Now telling someone you're an atheist can be tanta-
mount to telling someone you are a terrorist. I usually try to keep my beliefs to myself, but people do a
lot of talking about their gods. I find whether it's just
saying thank God all the time, or talking about Buddha, meditation, Temple, people are often referring
to their religion. If I am in a situation where I might
reveal that I am an atheist, first thing someone says
is, you mean agnostic? I say no, I mean atheist. I hate
agnostics, I mean, come on, you *doubt* the existence
of God? It's not like choosing steamed or pan-fried.
This is serious stuff. Then you have to put up with
their rounds of questions. Then what do you believe
in? How do you think we got here? Usually before I
offend anyone by saying I think you've got to be stupid, or in denial to believe in God, I say something
like, well this is a never-ending discussion, and then
try to change the subject. You always get one righ-
teous comment like I'll pray for you, or God loves
atheists too. I want to say fuck you and the God you
rode in on.

I'LL NEVER UNDERSTAND relationships. Not that I
have a lot to go on. Most people my age have been
married at least two or three times, or managed to
maintain a long-term marriage. I can't remember my

last date. I haven't heard from my first and only wife in fifteen years. My last serious relationship ended ten years ago. I lived with a butcher. No kidding. The problem is you can't argue with someone who's that good with a knife. Jill was one of those New Age women. She let her hair go gray at eleven. She didn't wear make-up. Not that any of that's a problem for me; I don't die my hair or wear make-up. She had a good sense of humor and only butchered organic meat. She burned incense and practiced a synthesis of paganism, Buddhism and consumerism. She had the most amazing hemp wardrobe imaginable, and a different meditation pillow for each day of the week.

Since then it's been clumsy dates. I don't have much money, so it's hard for me to take a woman out. Those two-for-one dinner specials don't impress. Nowadays it costs as much to cook at home as it does to take her out. Even coffee can be an expensive date if she orders one of those fancy things. For the past ten years I have lived mostly on spaghetti with garlic and olive oil. Sometimes I throw canned tuna in. My first wife Claire told me you're too irritable and controlling.

They say trust is everything in a relationship. Once you lose your trust, it's finished. I say no human being can be completely trusted. It's in our genes. If it was down to the last piece of food and it's you and another person—you'd say lookout and when they look you'd kick them in the balls and grab the food. Just make sure you kick as hard as you can.

The other day I spoke to a man in the convenience store near my apartment. He's an Egyptian immigrant who owns the store. He had a smudge of tuna salad, it could have been chicken, in his beard. It's a thick beard and some of the food had spread. He might have rubbed it not realizing it was there. We spoke for several minutes as we always do. A number of times I looked at the food in the beard, and nodded my head yes responding to what he said. At any moment during that time I could have stopped and politely said Allah (his name) you've got some food in your beard. But I didn't. Nor would I consider it. Trust. How can you trust humanity when it won't point out tuna salad in a beard?

I took a walk and sat in the park. I've had a lot of free time on my hands. An unseasonably warm day, Sunday, and all kinds of people out—families, lovers, and older folks. I saw a young woman walk through the park. She wore a sundress and its hem had somehow caught on her shoulder bag, so her entire left leg was exposed up past her thong. Being a swine, I took a quick but good look at what I will never again know the pleasures of. She stopped. By now other people sitting and milling about had noticed. She walked up to a couple and asked the time. "Five of three," as they watched her walk off with her flesh exposed. Later as I returned down the avenue I saw her again, her ass still on display as she made her merry way. Not one person with courage enough to tell her.

THERE'S NOTHING MORE annoying than those quaint philosophical quotations that get printed in the newspaper, or you see them on the Internet. Things like, what a man is, is much more than what a man has. They're usually from someone like Henry David Thoreau, or Teddy Roosevelt, or Helen Keller. No offence to the blind. I have nothing against the blind. In fact my therapist and my psychiatrist are both blind. It's got to be fate.

I can show up without combing my hair or wearing a clean shirt. If they ask me something that makes me uncomfortable—they can't see if I shift my body position. I've heard that a blind person has heightened senses, like smell. But I've also heard that's what stupid people say. Just to play it safe, I always shower before seeing either one of them. The biggest benefit in them not being able to see is that I can gyp them on the co-pay.

How many times has someone told you something making you swear that you will not tell anyone? Not another soul? Not even your husband or your wife or your girlfriend or boyfriend? How many times have you broken such a promise? I don't care who you are, somewhere along the line, you're out with some friends, having a couple of drinks, and suddenly you're saying, guys if I tell you something you have to swear that you won't tell it to anyone else. You'll swear on your mother's soul and to Saint Anthony and the Virgin Mary. You even swear to God. My Uncle Vinny used to say, May I die of cancer if I tell a soul, and the very next thing he'd be calling someone.

My mother was a simple woman. She tended mostly to my father's needs. She cooked, cleaned, and took his shit. She lived in her cloistered first generation world. Anything outside of it, that appeared foreign to her, that sounded different, looked different or smelled different, she would respond to by saying they say you can do it that way. I wanted peanut butter or baloney sandwiches. She said that's what the Americans eat. This confused me. Every day at school we pledged to the flag, sang America the Beautiful songs, practiced kneeling under our desks in case the Russians or Chinese might suddenly bomb us. I felt as American as my classmates. Why can't I have peanut butter or baloney? She made me eggplant on crusty Italian bread. The oil leaked through the wrapping and the paper bag. Other days I ate Italian tuna—the dark meat packed in olive oil—and it stunk up the classroom. Then there was the sandwich of ubiquitous salami and/or mortadella. And without fail a piece of fruit. Other kids ate canned soup out of thermoses, white tuna on white bread, peanut butter or baloney. They had cookies and other assorted packaged snacks for dessert. They would swap—two cookies for one cupcake, a brownie for a bag of chips. My pear was worthless in such a market.

I LIVE IN A rent controlled neighborhood. The rents are low because nobody wants to live here. Nobody with money that is. It's the kind of neighborhood where you still see cars up on milk crates. When I grew up lots of Italians lived here. A few are still around, but over the years as the old-timers have died off, their children sold and headed for the suburbs. Now it's folks from all over South America, and then some. The buildings are crowded together. There's too much concrete. Not enough trees. For a time it looked like things would change. Some of the nicer neighborhoods were being taken over by professionals, yuppies. One by one they encroached closer and closer. Property values were soaring. People turned houses over, reaping big returns in record time. It was crazy and out of control. Broken down old three-family homes got quick makeovers, and were sold floor by floor as condominiums at extraordinary prices. Everybody gouged.

Then the economy went down the drain and it all stopped. I hear there are apartments for rent all over the city. Everywhere I see For Sale signs and nothing's selling. The sign on the Charleston Chew Building that reads, Future Home of the Charleston Chew Building Lofts, is faded and peeling, hanging on the side of the old relic. Americans are so obsessed with money. It's the thing we value most— more important than ethics or morals or the quality of life. But we're no different from Spain or England or Portugal or France before us. I remember my Uncle Vinny, commenting on a friend of his who'd been arrested for having an affair with an underage girl. He could buy and sell us all, Uncle Vinny said. As far as he was concerned that's what mattered.

Who cares how you get it? Cheat, steal or lie— just as long as you don't get caught, and even if you do, we'll forgive you. For Christ's sake look at our royal family, the Kennedys. Where'd their fortune come from? Now old Ted's got brain cancer he can do no wrong. Why not open the files on Mary Jo? My mother loved John Kennedy. He was our greatest president, she said, because he was Catholic. My poor mother, she didn't even know that Protestants were Christians too. We buried Nixon a few years ago as if he'd been the second coming of Christ. Denial. If you believe in God you'll believe anything.

I work as a substitute teacher. The pay isn't much but all I have to do is call the school department and tell them I'm available. It's not that I'm a teacher, it's that I'm desperate for work, and they're desperate for someone desperate enough to watch a class for less then what a baby sitter makes. Today I taught, if you want to call it that, a first grade class. Mostly I just told kids to get in their seats because most of them ran around and did what they wanted to do. One boy came up to me and told me he had an accident. I didn't know what he meant until I smelled it. He does it every day, one of the other kids shouted. I do not, the boy said, and he started crying. I asked the boy did he think he needed to go to the bathroom and he said he goes to the nurse and she keeps extra pants for him.

This same boy's mother had come up to me before school started. She said that her son didn't eat meat. She also said that he didn't take any sugar because it wasn't a growth food. I don't know what a growth food is, but I nodded my head as if I did. She asked that I keep an eye out that he doesn't eat anything he shouldn't. I told her I'd try. She said that substitutes often showed movies and asked did I plan on showing any movies. I hadn't thought that far ahead, I explained. Her son didn't watch television, many children's movies weren't really appropriate, and if I do show a movie could her son go to another class with some work to do? I'd been in the school for ten minutes, rushed to the office to get my assignment, then out to the schoolyard to find the class running around like fiends because they'd already heard they had a substitute. With much difficulty I rounded them up and marched them to the class, and this mother had me stuck with my jacket still on yapping about her son's needs and her wants. What was a woman like this doing in Everett? No wonder her son shits his pants at school.

MOST PEOPLE aren't realistic enough when it comes to relationships. You read personal ads and look at the things that would-be lovers write down as impor- tant. Likes walking on the beach. Loves traveling and romantic dinners. Give me a fucking break. Who doesn't? What gives after that? A year or two or three—in the case of my marriage ten—years down the line where are those walks on the beach and romantic dinners? You've got to have something else to do in-between those times. If you live in a cold climate you probably can't even make it to the beach year round. Likes to be spontaneous. What does that mean? Run outside naked in a rainstorm? Jump on a plane for Madagascar? And people list their religion too. Christian and Jewish are biggies. Of course the Christians break it down: Protestant, Catholic, Bap- tist, Episcopalian ... There's an agnostic contingency, as well as Buddhists, pagans, and other assorted New Age theologies, and of course there are always a very few, the proud, the brave, the atheists. The saddest part about these ads are the women who write that they love watching football or baseball. How fuck- ing desperate does she have to be? It's like saying hey guys, I'll be just another one of your idiot buddies but you can fuck me. I know people say that's sexist, many women like sports these days. Maybe. I think if you were to submit them to a few seconds of water boarding they'd change their tune.

Is there anything more sickening than a couple falling in love? They're on about how from the first time I set my eyes on him I knew. The first night we met we talked all night as if we knew each other our entire lives, and bullshit like that. And the sex, the best ever and they do it morning noon and night. Give it some time. Give it two, or ten, or twenty years. The time it can take for everything in common to become little in common.

As a boy I fantasized about love and marriage and practiced kissing my pillow pretending it was Susan Marino. She was the first girl I ever whacked off to, and by sixth grade she had fully developed breasts. After I'd whack it I'd whisper sweet nothings in her ear, kiss my pillow and hold it close. How happy we could be. Walking the beach. Romantic dinners. Children. She ended up with Paul Tucci, he ended up throwing trash for the city. I never had kids. My wife didn't want kids. She had two with her second husband and when she married the third time she adopted one. My last real girlfriend, the butcher Jill, had a son. By the time she and I started dating he was nearly grown up and off to college. So I never experienced that kind of thing. I have nothing against kids, I think kids are nice, it's adults that I hate. Let's face it, kids are great, socialization fucks them up. Then when we grow up, we pay therapists, and tell them how our parents fucked us up. How fucked up is that? My father slapped me in the face for saying I thought Martin Luther King was a great man. How did that make me feel you ask?

HOW LONG HAVE you been doing this? How old are you I shot back. Twenty-eight he said. Longer than that I said. His unnaturally black hair looked as if someone had randomly hacked at it with a pair of scissors. He had lots of tattoos and rings on his nose, lips and ears. We'd gone outside when asked did I smoke pot. I hadn't for years but I didn't want this kid to think he had anything on me. I choked when I took my first hit. It's a splif he said, tobacco and weed mix. Two tokes and I became ecstatic. My body began to soar, my chest pounded and I felt a great swelling inside. What happened with pot? Where did the nickel bag go? The last time I bought some, it cost me over a hundred bucks and sold by the gram. We stood in the back of the club talking while he finished the rest.

You know, he said, you're a nice guy and I think you're funny. But if you don't mind me saying so, I think you go overboard with the God and religion stuff. I mean it's kind of been done to death. What

29

hasn't been done to death I asked? To my mind all the great ones were just making old material their own: Lenny Bruce, George Carlin, Richard Pryor, Moms Mabley. We'd watch her on Ed Sullivan's show on Sunday nights. My father was a fan as well. Something about how Moms had to edit and dumb her act down for Sullivan's white audience appealed to my father's idea of a funny black woman. This kid possessed all the arrogance that a twenty year old could muster. In a high-pitched tone while holding in a hit he said that he didn't have any use for most comedians. Same old same old he said blowing out the smoke. Like the religion and God stuff.

I quickly pointed to the fact that millions of people still believing we got it wrong about the dinosaurs means that we still need to laugh at religion. Then I pointed out to my new and very stoned friend that his bit was mostly about sex and what's been done in comedy more than that? Yeah, he paused, appeared to be deep in thought, then added that people always like sex. Sex, he paused and thought again, you know man it's primal. No, I wouldn't know. At least these days but I didn't tell him. But God, he paused again, God is dead. I mean God is dead, he's really dead, you know what I mean, man?

When I got home I sat up until early morning with a notebook and pencil writing down every marvelous and funny thing that came into my head. I fell off to sleep certain I'd come up with a stockpile of potential new material. I woke to find I'd eaten spaghetti with garlic and olive oil and I couldn't make sense of my previous night's scribbling.

THERE'S NOTHING WORSE than attending a family funeral or wedding. All my cousins are fat and old, just like me. Now that they know I live in the area again, I have to go. Especially since mother is unable and my sister lives in Vermont busy with her business. I'm the local representative of the family. Fortunately, most of the aunts and uncles are dead already. But now some of my cousins have dropped dead. At the wakes my living cousins ask things like do I remember the time we did this and do I remember the time we did that? As if something we did one afternoon forty-five years ago still has meaning. I have a cousin, the mob one in the bit, who always asks do I remember the time he had to take a shit when we were hanging out behind the schoolyard? I ran home to get a roll of toilet paper while he remained there crouched behind the school, his ass hanging un-wiped over the steamy pile. At a recent wedding he brought this up as we sat around a table eating prime rib. That was the longest five minutes I ever had, he said.

Everybody wants know where does the time go? How long has it been? Why am I still trying to do comedy if it hasn't happened by now? It's part of the

American way: status and money vs. quality of life. If you're not rich and famous, you aren't anybody. Nothing to be said about spending your life doing something you chose to do.

My parents never understood me doing comedy, even though my mother said I was always the clown. Oh they did for a short while when I had an agent and made a little money and did the cable show. All the aunts, uncles and cousins watched and my Uncle Vinny stopped talking to me because he knew the mafia-cousin in the bit to be his son. My Uncle Vinny always said he put a baby daughter in the crib and next thing he knew he married off a beautiful woman although the part about her being beautiful is stretching it some: they called Lucy, Faccia Brutta.

The last agents I contacted said the same thing. There's less and less work around. I'm a tough demographic: straight white male in his fifties. One agent I contacted told me point blank I was too old. That was it. I decided to go it on my own. What I lost I've made up with not having to pay an agent's fees. Either way it's not enough. The substitute money keeps the bill collectors away. Almost. In a few years I'll be drooling on my pajamas in some state run nursing home.

NORMAN IS MY oldest friend. I met Norman when I worked in a supermarket. He was a year older than me and we'd both started part-time while in high school. He stayed on part time while he went to college and I worked full-time. I began as a cashier but moved into the aisles filling in where needed. Eventually I ended up working produce under the revered department manager Freddy Pisappia. Norman worked produce too and we got to know each other. He was putting himself through college and encouraged me. I was looking for an apartment and a way out of my parent's house at the time. You're a pretty smart guy, he said. Have you ever thought about going to college? I really hadn't. Working here is fine right now, I said. I'd be happy to have Freddy's job some day. But you might not want to be here thirty years down the road, Norman said. Norman is a lawyer. A good one. What I mean is, he went into law to help people. Norman is recovering from his own bankruptcy and paying bills by taking advantage of the surplus of bankruptcy cases due to the tanking economy. Norman is generous and he lends money out. He's passed a little my way on more than one occasion and rarely gets paid back. He's been married four times and says that no one can live with him, and for that matter, he can't live with anyone for more than five years. It's just not meant to be Norman says. Recently he lent his third wife two thousand dollars. Or maybe it was his second wife three thousand dollars. Sometimes we meet for coffee or lunch and Norman usually picks up the check.

Norman had himself snipped after his second marriage. He hates kids. Or should I say he hates people. Norman says most people live with blinders on because it's comfortable. The last thing he wants to be guilty of is bringing another idiot into the world. I often point out that his cynicism doesn't fit with his idea of himself using law to help people. If people suck the way Norman often—in fact always emphatically states—why try to help them? Like all of us, Norman stands on shifting sands. The last time Norman got divorced he made me promise him that I would take a gun and put it to his head if he ever talked about marrying again. But there's nothing I can do. Love is like God. Denial rules.

TODAY I VISITED my mother. I found her wandering the hallway of the unit, confused, wearing a jacket and carrying her empty purse. She didn't recognize me right away and assumed I was one of the attendants. I need to go to the bathroom, she said. I took her by the hand and led her to her room. When she came out of the bathroom I asked her would she like to go out for a walk and maybe lunch. She didn't understand. You mean here, she wanted to know. It took several minutes until she figured out what I meant. Oh yes, she said. I can't stand it here. They had the television on so loud and it's the same movie all the time I got a headache. I signed her out and we drove down to the ocean at Lynn Shore Drive. I parked where I've been parking for years, when she had her apartment, her own car, we'd walk up to the Nahant Circle and back then eat a big lunch at one of the local Chinese restaurants.

It came slow in increments, made it easy to normalize until the bigger things—car accidents, wandering away during a walk, forgetting names and places, water faucets left running, gas burners that could have caused fires, falls. We walked a little bit. I know this place, she said. Have you ever been here before? she asked me. I told her yes many times we used to walk all the way to Nahant Circle do you remember oh yes she said, sure. So you've been here before she asked again? We sat down on a bench and watched the people taking advantage of one of the first good spring days—they walked dogs, rollerbladed, jogged, strolled, pushed carriages with newborn babies in them. Why do I have this on? my mother asked, pointing to the electronic ankle bracelet. I didn't have that before. Yes you have I said. What's it for? So they can keep track of you. I can tear it off she said. Why would you want to do that I asked? Then I told her it was too strong she couldn't tear it. I can cut it she replied. I changed the subject and told her that Anna was coming down to visit her next week. You know Anna she asked? Of course I said she's my sister. Anna is your sister? Yes I told her. Anna is your daughter and I am your son so Anna is my sister. I didn't know that she said.

I took her to the Chinese restaurant we've been going to for years. I ordered her usual wanton soup and shrimp with vegetables with the two chicken fingers. I splurged and had a seafood noodle soup. My sister Anna sends me a check once a month in case I should want to take my mother out for lunch or buy her some chocolates. She can eat an entire box in a day. I cut her wantons and she fidgeted with the soupspoon and slowly worked her way through the cup of soup. Her main course sat on the table for nearly ten minutes while she finished the soup. I guiltily looked up at the clock, minutes passed in silence. I asked how is she sleeping and how she is eating? Does she remember Sunday mornings and cooking? She looked at me as if I struck a chord. Oh yes she said, that was a long time ago. Do you remember dad I asked her? She thought for a moment. A long time ago she said. Did you like him? I struck another chord. She looked at me perplexed. C'mon tell the truth I urged, did you like him? Not really she said. She kept getting her silverware confused so that she couldn't get food into her mouth so I cut everything up and told her to eat it with her soup spoon. At one point she took my cup of tea and poured it over her food saying that the sauce is good. She asked where's the band? What band? She heard

36

the piped-in traditional Chinese music. It's coming from the speakers, I pointed. She looked confused. I think they're outside the window she said pointing to the computer screen in the waiter station. That's not a window I said. What is it? It's a computer screen. A what? She didn't want to go back she said. She wanted her old house. All they do is sleep there she lamented, her voice rose abruptly when she added that one lady keeps showing her pussy. I'd never heard her use that word in such a way. The people at the next table looked at us. They had two children with them and I apologized.

She wanted to know when we got back to the home where we were. I explained that this was where she lived. Probably she said. I left her in the recreation room. They were getting ready for the afternoon movie. The patients were inching their way across the room, in wheelchairs, with walkers, on foot. One woman repeatedly sang show me the way to go home, I'm tired and I want go home. I could smell shit and pee. A woman sitting in a wheelchair grabbed my arm. The attendant shouted for her to let me go. When the woman didn't, the attendant came over and pulled her hand away, scolding her to keep her hands to herself. Driving home I felt guilty for not visiting my mother enough. I imagined myself in her place twenty or thirty years down the road and no one to visit me. By the time I was halfway home she forgot I'd been there.

Lolli Pop had lovely straight blond hair, shoulder length, a sheen that can only come out of a bottle. Except for her protruding Adam's apple you could have fooled me. She told tranny jokes and how there's nothing lower on the ladder when you tell someone you are a tranny. She had a funny bit about a class reunion. I would disagree with her about being a tranny and say atheists are lower on the ladder. Imagine what it must be like for an atheist tranny?

There were a number of other tranny people in the audience who were there to see Lolli. Before long I found myself spying on every woman. Who were the real women? Is a trans a real woman after she goes through all the proper procedures? Someone told me they remove the penis and build a vagina with plastic surgery. I had a feeling my raunchier stuff would work and I was right. Anything about sex, porn, anal sweat juices, got a laugh. I did my bit about how men are never too old to want sex and there's a porn site online called Oxyblow.com featuring photos and movies of dying men hooked up to oxygen machines getting blowjobs. I got carried away with porn. It's easy to do when you're horny and lonely and you have way too much time on your hands. I hit bottom when I didn't come up for air for eight days. I missed a gig. Later my right arm needed physical therapy. I lied of course and told them I'd twisted it doing push-ups. I call it my lost eight-day weekend.

In terms of masturbation it's important to have a strong team. You've got stars, the ones who come through in more ways than one and deliver the goods whenever you need them. But you also need a strong bench. You find yourself going off your favorites sometimes. You start playing the second stringers, or breaking in a rookie. That's always fun, especially if it's someone you've known for a while. You know someone and they never seem sexy to you. Then suddenly one day, bang, they're hitting the ball out of the park. Or you see a person you haven't seen in years, a person who used to be on your team but had fallen out of the rotation or who never was on your team and suddenly you want them to play for you. And all the members of the team should get along and be interchangeable so that on any given stroke they can shift positions. After all it is your fantasy team. And how many of you have people on your team who you don't even like in real life? I find that can be very useful when you get to the kinkier innings, you know the ropes and cat-o-nine-tails.

MY FATHER always said—he got it from my Uncle Vinny who got it from my grandfather—you've got to straighten the tomato plant when it's young or it will grow crooked. My silliness was ok in the right time and right place. I was always the one making a face when the camera was on me. The old home movies

39

we're all standing in front of our Medford house and the rose bush is in bloom I'm wearing my white First Holy Communion outfit, making faces, putting my hands in my mouth and crossing my eyes, doing a kind of soft-shoe shuffle for the camera. Or the photo of my sister's Confirmation all of us around the table and I put the salad bowl over my head. It was worth the smack in the face I got from my father as Uncle Vinny snapped the photo. I wonder where it ended up.

I couldn't stop goofing off. In boy scouts I led a group on knot-tying and we tied up a scout and stuffed him in the troop's rope box. In band the music teacher called my parents because I interrupted class by sneaking in notes out of order. In school I was the kid passing notes and shooting spitballs. I lived for the next laugh. I rigged my pen so that it could be converted in moments to a lethal spitball shooter. I stored spit-moistened paper balls in the inside corner of my desk and in twenty seconds could assemble my weapon, blow off several rounds and put my pen back together. Only Patrick Skinner and I had the nerve to target beyond the nerdy kids in class. We'd hit the jocks and other cool kids if we could get away with it. We were known for scoring hits on teachers. I once ricocheted one off my French teacher's desk and it stuck right on her glasses. The class celebrated me for days.

One time in sixth grade my teacher called my parents about my difficult behavior. I told my father that the teacher had me wrong, that I wasn't doing all the things she'd accused me of. One day, unbeknownst to me, my father snuck in to class and watched me from behind the coatroom. Patrick Skinner and I were on a roll, passing notes, assaulting Stephen Caruso with spitballs—a perfect target. He picked his nose, rolled his snots then examined them before pressing the booger-balls under his desk where they'd stick and dry. I took a look at those works of art on a dare from Skinner. I had just placed a spitball on Caruso's cheek when suddenly my teacher Miss Bagnuglio, known as Bags, said to my father who appeared from the coatroom, I hope you see what I mean now. I sure do he said. And when I get him home, he's going to get a beating to remember.

Those were the days when you could say you were going to beat your kid in front of a teacher. That school day never seemed to end. I didn't want it to. My father's wrath came usually in the form of taking down my pants and getting strapped four or five or six times while he shouted. At lunch Patrick Skinner asked would my father really do what he said he was going to do and I assured him he would. That afternoon my father didn't get home until around five and I had to wait. He called me into the living room and started working himself up, removing his belt, shouting how I had no respect for him and the teacher and I had lied. He didn't make me take off my pants just swung the strap wildly catching me on the arms or

41

the top of my head and one swipe on the cheek that left a mark. The pants-down method left welts but you couldn't see them.

So he straightened the tomato plant. Within weeks I was back to my old antics at school. In-between these events my father tried to keep me in line with sayings like you haven't had a beating in a while, or if I have to get called up to school one more time I'll break your legs. As a boy in Italy during WW II my father gambled the buttons off his only shirt. He'd switch price tags in stores. Once while buying me a baseball bat the cashier caught it, and pointed out to him that the bat was more money than marked. He turned to me and asked do I still want it. What do you do when you're twelve and you realize your father is a slime bucket?

AFTER ALL IT's the adults who mess up the purity of the kids. Today at the school—I had a third grade class—a boy bit off another boy's ear. Not the whole ear but a corner of the lobe. It seems the boy whose ear was bitten bit the boy who bit him first. That's what witnesses say. And the boy who bit the boy's ear off also had teeth marks from the boy he'd bitten, in his arm. The first boy had said to the second boy who happens to be Chinese-American that Chinese people are ugly. The boy who made the comment is Hispanic. So the Chinese boy bit the Hispanic boy.

The Hispanic boy bit off the Chinese boy's lobe. By the time it was all sorted out and both boys taken to the hospital for shots and stitches, they were out of teacher's salads in the cafeteria, an excellent deal for $2.45 that includes lots of fresh vegetables and grilled chicken. I ate cold plastic-tasting chicken tenders, pissed that my lunch had been cut short and cursing the two boys in question for costing me my teacher's salad.

Where does it come from? Where did one boy first hear that a certain kind, type, race, color, creed, is ugly? I remember in 1963 my fourth grade teacher saying there were so many Chinese people, that if they all stood up on a bench at the same time and jumped down they could cause a worldwide earthquake more damaging than an atomic bomb. This was my fourth grade teacher. We were nine years old. When a black couple came to look at the second floor apartment my parents were renting out, my father told them it had already been rented. Now we have an African-American president. People say things have changed.

The other day during a youth soccer game in Connecticut a father ran out on the field and punched a boy. The nine year old had scored six goals against his son's team. It seems the father had been harassing the rival team's coach to take the star out of the game and make it fair. The coach ignored the man so the angry father took matters into his own hands.

Police arrested the man who asked what ever happened to good sportsmanship. It's all about winning now. Any way you can. Cheat. Lie. Steroids. Just get to that winner's circle. Did you win? How did you do? We smashed them. We crushed them. We blew them away. We wiped the field with them. We we we I never understand what we means. You watch the news and there's a fan saying we're number one or we kicked butt no you didn't the team did you are not on the team. You don't do how was the ballet? Oh, we were just brilliant! How was the concert? We were marvelous you should have heard our violin solo in D flat/minor.

I hate sports. I tried. I went to games. Played a little baseball, relegated to right field for two innings where I stood watching birds and butterflies, hoping that nobody hit the ball in my vicinity. Somewhere along the way I remember it was a hazy weekend summer afternoon and I sat in front of the television watching a game and it came over me like a revelation: this has got to be one of the most boring things on the planet. All the endless interruptions, commercials, time wasted between pitches and foul balls, the banter between the announcers. But there must be something wrong with me I thought. Millions of people all over the world watch sports, cheer for their teams, waste endless hours of free time glued to television sets and radios. Millions and millions of sports fans can't be wrong. My salvation came with the knowledge that millions and millions of people around the world believe in a God.

I'll be glad when this fitness craze is over. It's gone way too far. You see them on television, men and women, marbled specimens promising that you too can look like they do by using the new flexi-spring twenty minutes a day three times a week. Call now you get the colon rinse kit to flush out unwanted toxins. The only way anyone could look the way the people on television look is by working out four hours a day, eating a special diet, and remaining under forty years of age. Why would people want to work eight or ten hours a day on a job and then go to a gym to workout and punish themselves? You see them at night—why are gyms always on the second floor—through the big windows in those brightly lit rooms, sitting on machines, lifting, running in place, cycling with those headphone things on—like they're running for their lives. You can't outrun death. Who is to say they wouldn't be better off saving their money and spending it on ice cream or beer? No amount of plastic surgery or gym memberships can stop the black sneakers from squeaking.

I'll tell you what really makes me sick are those jogger moms with the specially equipped carriages. Those poor women aren't allowed to miss a beat, have the baby then got to get that body right back into television shape, don't want the hubby to have a reason to start cruising the gym. You see them struggling along, pushing carriages with three big wheels talking to their babies in the same sickening tone they use with their dogs. Precious enough to make you fucking puke. It's still a man's world I think. Though things are evening up a bit. Now guys have to be buff too. Remember when guys could look like shit and get the beautiful woman? Though the other day I heard some ugly fat guy say something like yeah, she's cute but she's got small tits. Excuse me have you looked in the mirror lately? You're ugly and you've got big tits. I got 'em too. The man boobs. In the last ten years they're grown two cup-sizes. I'm very self-conscious about them and it's one more reason to remain celibate. Everybody's got to be beautiful. Rich and beautiful is even better. Rich, famous and beautiful is best.

The last person I asked out was my tax accountant. I only saw her once a year, but there's something intimate about being that close at the desk, my personal information displayed on her computer screen. The first year she did my taxes she pointed out that we were born the same day. Mutual conversation led to the discovery we'd grown up one city apart. I figured her as gay. She had short dark hair, wore dark tops, black jeans, cowboy boots and funky earrings. She smelled of cigarette smoke and laughed heartily when I said funny things. Some would consider her a little chubby and butch. Not me. Of course I'm a little chubby myself. She lived year round on a boat, alone. I liked her wit.

By the third year I had a full-blown crush, and made my appointment earlier than ever. On this visit my hopes were raised when she referred to a male friend several times. Maybe she isn't gay after all. The fourth year I planned on asking her out and letting the chips fall where they may. I waited the entire hour and a half for the right time but it never came. Or it came and I missed it. No matter, I had her card and would phone. Twice during the next week I phoned but hung up before I got an answer. The fifth year I asked her out. Five minutes into our meeting she hadn't even popped my previous year's return up on the screen. Before I miss the chance, I said, because I've been waiting a year to ask, would you go out with me some time? Oh, I'm flattered she said. But I just met someone about six months ago and we've been seeing a lot of each other. Besides that I'm gay. You seem like a nice guy though.

I wanted to get up and run out of the office. But I couldn't. She had all my official tax stuff in her hands. I sat there, dazed as she explained various details pointing to the computer screen, so you can see how much less you made this year from last. I wanted to crawl into myself and die when she told me that I almost qualified for food stamps. She con-tacted me around tax time the next year with phone calls and a note. I went to H&R Block and have ever since.

LAST NIGHT I went after the Catholics. My first gig in three weeks, and I alienate half the audience. The first act was a ventriloquist, a young woman perhaps a student form the nearby college, many in the crowd knew her. I like the idea of an African-American woman with a white male dummy in a blue suit, white shirt and red tie, but the material was predictable, though the audience laughed on cue. Nonetheless when I saw her later I smiled and she averted her eyes. Maybe she was a Catholic.

I opened with stuff about my mother. How she always prefaced nouns with the adjective nice. I made some nice soup. I bought some nice broccoli. I'm frying up some nice cutlets. I made some nice lemonade. Anything that didn't figure into her tiny world she would dismiss with her proverbial they say you can do it that way. Ma, you don't have to take the back road, there's a highway. Oh, they say you can go that way. She never had a dishwasher, insisting that she wash them herself. She scrubbed floors and walls. Washed laundry and dishes while my father ran around with women or sat in on the latest card game. She never missed Mass. Every Sunday morning she'd get up early, get the Sunday morning sauce going with the meatballs, sausages, braciole, and go to the ten o'clock Mass at Saint Francis of Assisi Church. At least God loves me she said.

The nuns in Sunday school told us that only Catholics could get into heaven. They explained all the ins and outs of purgatory and hell. Being so young, it was hard to understand what burning in hell for eternity meant, eventually wouldn't you just burn up and there'd be nothing left? One thing for sure, if you weren't a Catholic, you weren't getting into heaven. Sunday school should have been called Thursday-afternoon school because that's when we went. It's where the public school kids got their religious schooling. Once, one of the nuns accused me of writing fuck on the desk. It had to have been me she insisted, a Catholic school student would never have done it. All I knew is that I didn't do it, but she called my mother anyway and my father gave me a strapping. It's that crime and punishment thing. Notice all the pain and suffering that go along with Christianity? I remember that same nun telling us about Jesus carrying his own cross, getting whipped along the way, she placed her palms in the air and continued, they put spikes through Jesus' flesh and bones she said as she stretched her arms out to imitate him hanging on the cross. For three days he hung there she said—no food, no water, bleeding and sweating, the endless pain. Then he died. She took a deep breath, reopened her eyes and said, and he rose to heaven. I believe that Sister Hot Bloomers had an orgasm during her reenactment. But there's a bright side to all this suffering. He did it for me, for my sins, so that I can be forgiven. Could there be anything sicker than the concept of baptism? That some precious newborn baby is born in sin, and has to be cleansed?

I remember when my father died at the funeral Mass the priest said my father was a good man. My father was in heaven with God now. The priest knew nothing about my father. He lied to the people in the church. If they'll lie to a group of mourners, they'll lie to anyone about anything. The last time I went to a Mass the last aunt on my mother's side died. It doesn't matter if you haven't gone in ten or twenty years, Mass is the same. It doesn't change. There's nothing blander than the mumble of the white man's shout and response. The Lord be with you. And also with you. Let us give him thanks and praise. It is right to give him thanks and praise. The Catholic Church is closing area churches down. It's revenge. They'll never get over losing their child sex ring.

I HEAR THAT Facebook is great you connect with all these people from your past, and present, and they share their stuff and you share yours. I understand you use photos, too. Here's Phil, horseback riding last week. And here's the mother with the newborn Brady, nine pounds three ounces. And here's Janice and her grandchildren with the family cat. I don't want to get in touch with people from my past. It's taken me fifty-three years to shake them. Other than Norman and my sister, there's no one else I need to call, or care to call, or send a photo to. I still have a single lens reflex camera. There's been nothing I want to take a picture of for years. I don't care what Jimmy Meloni is doing now. I don't want to see Nancy Testa, sitting on the new deck with her granddaughter.

I've always been a fan of commercial free radio, and take advantage of the local college radio programming. There's a wide variety of music to be heard, and the stations often have promotion tickets available for various events. On any given day, the disc jockeys give away tickets for a movie, musical, comedy or dance performance. I call for tickets now and again, and if I win, I often take Norman. He appreciates it and buys drinks or dinner. The older I get, the less I want to go out. Sometimes I win tickets, then change my mind and don't use them.

Everybody in my family used to talk loudly, excitedly, wave their hands to conduct their intent. Some people think I exaggerate in my routine but they don't know me. If I get my jaw flapping enough, I could side-smack someone. Claire couldn't live with it. Why are you shouting she always asked me? I'm not shouting I'm talking I would say, and then we'd argue and I'd end up really shouting. But where I grew up, everybody shouted. People shouted at the dinner table. They shouted on the phone, waving their hands as if the person on the other end of the line can see. They shouted out their windows. They shouted on the street. Maria, how are you? Good, how's your mother? The old men shouted in smoky cafés drinking espresso. The first time I brought my ex-wife Claire home to dinner she became shell-shocked. She thought we were all fighting, and later said it was the most unnerving experience she'd ever had. My father wore those Italian t-shirts. He'd wear them with holes, and that first time Claire came to dinner, my father tossed the salad and a hair from his woefully hairy body wound up in her salad. That garnish put a curse on my marriage.

I NEVER REALIZED what class was until I left Medford. I always thought we were middle class. The first time one of my friends had a car we all piled in and took a ride. This would be our pastime for the next several years. Pitch in for some gas, hop in someone's car, and get the fuck out of Medford. Didn't matter where we went. We'd drive through downtown Boston, or to Revere Beach, or out into the suburbs where there were single-family houses bigger than the two and three-family houses that we lived in. Large yards surrounded the homes, groomed lawns, shrubs, gardens, tall old pines and hardwood trees. How do you get here? I wanted to know. One of my friends said, What are you talking about? Look around you I said, look at these houses and these yards and the cars in the driveway. Think about where we live. How do you get here from where we live? You drive, you fucking idiot, that's what my friend said.

My Uncle Vinny used to brush his teeth with soap. He always said what's the difference as long as it gets them clean? When my father first came to this country, he worked with my Uncle Vinny doing construction. But as my Uncle Vinny always said, my father and hard work don't get along. Funny thing for my Uncle Vinny to say since he himself chose an early retirement. My father did some of the usual immigrant jobs, laborer, kitchen work, driving cab, driving truck. Later, through one of his connected friends, he landed a job working for the state in a parking garage downtown. He was a parking lot attendant and loved it. The work was easy, there were good benefits, and he took advantage of everything he could in terms of sick days and vacations days. Once he boasted that he hadn't worked a five-day week in three months. Somehow he made enough for us to live on, as long as he didn't gamble too much. Most of the time he had a budget and he tried to stick to it. Other times he'd go into a tailspin. He kept it all to himself if he won. It wasn't like he came home with toys for the kids or dresses for my mother. He dropped dead at sixty-three, figuring the dog track form, cigarette dangling from his mouth.

When I was growing up we ate too much. Both my parents and other people in the extended family knew what it is to starve. When they had the opportunity to eat heartily, they got carried away. Anything that they ate in the old country, my family would eat here. In the old country nothing went to waste. So in addition to the nice cuts of beef and chickens and pork, we also ate things like tripe and pig knuckles. One of the most celebrated foods didn't have a name that translated into English. The dried, salted pig-skin, reconstituted in water then filled with various goodies like cheeses, herbs, pine nuts, dried fruit, was rolled, seared in a frying pan, and simmered in the sauce for several hours. My father could eat a half a pound at a sitting. Even after his first heart attack he ignored all medical warnings and continued his overeating and smoking.

I think every man has his poison. It could be drugs, sex or booze, or gambling, or work, or money, vanity, physical fitness. I think sobriety and celibacy are a kind of poison too, though arguably healthier. I used to smoke cigarettes. I began smoking as a teenager and didn't quit until I was about 40. I was a pack-and-a-half-a-day man. The young kids are smoking now. I think it's because their parents come from the generation that stopped. They smoke those roll-your-own things and special organic tobacco stuff. Smoke is smoke. I recently read an article about smoking, they broke smoking down by class. The lower the class, the higher the rate of smokers.

AT NORMAN'S URGING I went to a cattle call for a show I've never heard of, where contestants perform on television in front of a live audience and a panel of three has-beens, or never-weres. The panel and live audience vote to decide the contestants' fate. I had nothing to lose, Norman said, and besides, what else did I have to do? Several hundred people were lined up outside the downtown building when I arrived. Men and women of every size and age, professionals and rank amateurs alike, stood waiting for a shot at the big time—each one of them certain of his or her particular genius. Officials at the door handed out numbers from one to six. I was handed a four and instructed to go inside, and get in line where I found about a hundred people ahead of me. I did the math, and considering the odds, I knew I didn't want to wait two hours to do one minute.

I decided that I would splurge and buy myself lunch. I went to a Tibetan joint that had a reasonably priced buffet. Buffets are ideal because I can really load up. I sat there, eventually to the chagrin of the waitress who kept coming to clear away my empty plate, as I rose to fill a clean dish with more food, and refill my cup with tea. Finally at two they started taking down the buffet. I'd eaten so much I struggled to get out of my chair. All afternoon I kept burping up all those spices and herbs.

Last night I lay in bed, tossing and turning, burping and farting. I couldn't get the images of the audition out of my mind. All of those people vying for a few measly openings. Many of them talented, most of them talent-less souls who should be sprayed over with a sleeping spray and put out of their misery. There were tens of thousands of us around the country who somehow think we're special and we have something funny to say. And we should be rich and famous and loved. It's good the world needs substitute teachers. The rich and famous will never happen for me if it hasn't yet. What else do I have? Childless. My only sister lives hundreds of miles away. As a young man I dreamed of my future and never thought I'd be here clinging to my joke of a career. I became overcome with anxiety and fear. I sat up and watched the weather station on television. There was rain one place, strong winds in another, drought in yet another. Near dawn a new weatherperson took over. It started to rain outside. I fell asleep and didn't wake until noon.

WHO WOULD EVER have thought we'd see a black president? I remember as a boy watching riots on television. Police chasing black protesters with dogs. Power hoses dispersing crowds of black people. My father said that Martin Luther King was only good for starting riots then running away. Where did those white people go? The ones who were burning crosses, and bombing churches, and killing young black men? Many of them are probably still here, collecting social security now. And their children live on. What did they hear around the dinner table from their elders? Have they all, every one, seen the light, these good Christian folks, and in one generation realized we are all children of God who we thank on Sunday afternoons for our peach pie?

It seems like the next world war could break out anywhere at any time. North Korea, Pakistan, the African continent, Gaza, South America. All over the planet there are big wars, little wars, long-time feuds, hatreds, resentments, continual skirmishes, battles, deaths and injuries. Sounds like marriage. Who wants to travel? I recently read an article about a dangerous situation in northern Ontario. A civil war is on the brink between bait fisherman and fly fisherman. Last week a man and his son were shot at as the son reeled in a trophy-size rainbow trout he hooked on a size-six hook and a night crawler. A group calling itself The Right To Fish Pure claimed responsibility. Many bait fishermen retaliated by shooting up every Toyota Landrover in the province—there were only three—and they had to belong to fly fisherman commented one bait fisherman who preferred to remain anonymous.

What's with farmer's markets? I have nothing against supporting local farmers and buying good produce. Problem is I don't have sixteen dollars to buy three carrots and an apple. What's most sickening about these farmer's markets is how precious we make them. It can't be just a produce market like in Europe where in the city you can go on any give day and purchase fresh produce from the countryside. We've got live brunch jazz, or new age folk singers. You can buy leather goods, jewelry, trinkets, overpriced baked goods, sixteen-dollar per pound hamburger, expensive jams and jellies, bread. Aging white Baby Boomers dance to the beat of conga drums. It's here in America at the farmer's market. Fridays from 2–4. Arrive early for a free raffle ticket. Bring your kids for free face-painting.

IF MY ADULT LIFE can be viewed as on a graph, during my thirties you can see the only sharp increase when I got married and had a potential career. It took me nearly six years to finish college in my twenties. I kept switching majors, or never really had one. Finally an advisor assessed my transcripts and told me that if I took one more political science course, I could take a degree in political science. This seemed odd since I had no interest in political science, and wasn't aware that so many of the courses I'd taken were in that major. So I took the course and got my degree.

During my student years I earned a living working part time at the supermarket. I lived at home and eventually took out some loans so I could move out. I couldn't take living with my parents any longer, and I needed my own place in case I should find a girl to have sex with. When I finally graduated I looked around for more serious work, something with normal hours and good pay and I'd wear a suit to work, like I went to college for. Or so I guessed. But I really didn't have a clue what to do with a political science degree. It was the 1970s during a recession. I went full time at the market and became assistant manager in produce. Freddy Pisappia now managed his own store. I worked under the taskmaster Bob Wilson.

One night some co-workers and I went out to a local bar after work. It was a comedy open mic. I remember that night thinking that none of the people were funny, and I could do that. In fact, I had a strange, foreign urge to do it. People always said that I was funny. As far back as I remembered I liked to make people laugh. During that week I began thinking about funny things I could say, and returned to the open mic. It was nothing like I'd imagined. I quickly discovered that standing in front of people, with lights on you, and three long minutes to fill wasn't like pulling Peggy Gianfelice aside at the market and telling her a penis joke in front of the bananas, or making prank calls about products we don't carry to the newcomer in canned goods.

Nonetheless I began to obsess, and returned week after week. Somewhere and somehow things began to fall, however slowly, into place until I had a few real bits down. I began going to other open mics, and eventually had my first feature that paid. People from the supermarket would come out and cheer me on. A few of my old friends from Medford too. Norman would bring one of his wives or new girlfriends. Five or so years later I signed with an agent. You'll never have to work in a supermarket again he promised, as the local media hyped a new comedy renaissance in Boston.

I met Claire not long after that. She was tall, fair skinned, carried herself elegantly in the way a Medford girl never could. And I'd never known anyone as smart. Claire had acted, sung in bands, played the flute and was finishing graduate school in library studies. She told me that night, emphatically, that she was an atheist. I fell in love. Within a few weeks we were living together in a basement apartment in Cambridge. My life seemed a million miles away from my youth in Medford, just two towns over. I'd never met a woman like Claire before. She was a long way from Tina Zamboni.

I think they were good times. We were close. I remember how often she would open her arms for a hug. We did a lot of hanging out together, listening to music, going out to see movies and hear live music. The sex was always good, if you measure it by quality not quantity. We loved the same things, and hated the same things, it seemed. Later, Claire said it was no fun for her. I had always been difficult to be around. She'd always felt tension, and at times, smothered. We got to travel a lot. I had gigs and for five or six years earned some decent money. There were down times if I had to go out of town without her. That wasn't the problem she said, I was overbearing, opinionated, moody and it always had to be my way. She felt that if she tried to express these things to me, I wouldn't listen. And I was always yelling, she said. I'm not yelling I told her.

As time went on it became apparent that we suddenly had differences, or we'd been blind to them all along. I hated that she liked to socialize. She'd make plans for us to spend time with friends of hers. I wanted quiet time together at home. She didn't want children. I did. During my thirties my depression became more noticeable, and at Claire's urging I sought help. But it was too late for us. One day I came home from being away for two days, and she told me it was over. The past months had been very shaky between us. I tried to dissuade her over the next weeks, but she'd made up her mind and had already secured a job in a library at a major university in Chicago.

AT AGE SEVEN I readied for my First Holy Communion—the first time in my life I tasted the body of Christ, in the form of a wafer. First Holy Communion is the second in a series of sacraments, baptism being first. I remember my parents rented me a white suit and white shoes. I had my photo taken, rosary beads in my praying hands. But before I could walk down the aisle and receive a taste of my savior, I had to first confess and be clear of sin.

Those weeks leading to the big event the nuns drilled us hard. We practiced confessional procedures: what to say, when to say it. Why so important to confess to God? We would confess all: there were venial sins and mortal sins, but God forgave. The priest, being the human representative of God, would give us a penance in the form of prayers we would say at the altar. I feared that I might sin between confession on Saturday and Mass on Sunday. Did God give you any leeway? What if I did sin in-between confession and communion? What if I didn't tell the priest all my sins? I swore twice, I told him. I lied to my parents once. Anything else he wanted to know. Not that I could think of. Say three of the Lord's Prayer and three Acts of Contrition.

And I knelt at the altar staring up at the stained glass and violent images, the extravagant crucifix looming over everything, candles glowing, smell of incense, Stations of the Cross showing Christ in various stages of punishment and humiliation.

When I was twelve I made my third sacrament. Confirmation. This is when you become an adult in the church. My parents made me do it. I never told them I no longer believed in God. Besides, they lied about Santa Claus. That day before Confirmation would be the last time I ever went to confession. As soon as I heard his voice I knew it was Father Tom, the newest priest in the parish. I'd never had him for confession, mostly because I skipped it. I gave him the usual I swore and I-lied-to-my-parents routine. Are you sorry for having done those things, he asked. Yes, I answered, I am. What about girls, he asked, do you ever think about girls? I gave him an uneasy no. Are you sure? I didn't answer. Do you ever touch yourself, he inquired? I knew all my friends were doing it, so there was nothing to be ashamed of. In God's eyes it was wrong. But there was no God. Yes, I told him, I have. How often he wanted to know? I remained silent. How often, he asked? I don't know, I answered. Once a day, twice a day, he continued his inquest. Twice a week, I said. When you touch yourself, do you think of girls? Yes, I answered. Do you ever think of boys when you touch yourself? Something about his tone, it changed. No, I replied. Are you sure you never think of boys? Yes, I'm sure I told him. It ended there. He lectured me on the evils of thinking of girls and touching myself, gave me my penance, and I left the church without going to the altar to say it.

I CAN FIND a few gigs during the summer but I have to travel. The clubs down Cape Cod, or up at the beach towns like Hampton and Salisbury, still book stand-ups. But there are few of the old clubs around, and more people looking for gigs. Twenty years ago I even headlined some of the joints like Timmy's Patio, The Beachcomber or The Wharf. Last night I opened for Eddie Wallace. Eddie fucking Wallace. The guy's as funny as a dial tone. He wasn't funny twenty years ago, and he's not funny now. But Eddie Wallace wasn't the headline, he was the special guest. Daisy Harris is a beautiful, young woman, daughter of a black man from Harlem, and a Manhattan socialite. Her material centers on her confused identity, childhood, incidents between her mother's family and her father's family. Daisy's built quite a following with cable specials and appearances on some television shows. By the time she went on, the room was packed.

When I took the stage, a few people were scattered about the big room. The front tables were empty, reserved for people who were probably dining at some nice restaurant that very moment, only interested in

Daisy. I started in about the recently released Richard Nixon tapes, his comments about abortion. He opposed it of course, except for instances of rape or interracial sex. Hmm. I am not a crook. A man who would look into a nation's eyes and lie.

I once caught my parents having sex. The image of the two of them I take to my death. I had bad dreams when I was a kid. The doctor said I had an overactive mind. I would wake up and racing thoughts would prevent me from getting back to sleep. Sometimes I would call for my mother or father. One of them would come in and settle me down. My father just wanted me to get back to sleep. He'd say, okay, put your head on your pillow and go back to sleep, don't be a baby. My mother would stay for a while, wrap her arms around me, and tell me stories about her life when she was a girl. That night I walked in on them, I woke from a dream, startled, out of breath. I'd been stuck in the bottom of a well, and after struggling to get out, had given myself up for dead. I ran to their bedroom and opened the door without knocking. He was on top of her. Go back to bed they barked in unison. At that time I had an idea what adults got up to, but the thought of my parents getting up to it made me sick.

Now that school's out I have a lot less money. My apartment is air conditioned but small. Sitting around, day in and day out, can get to me. I listen to music. I have thousands of recordings, vinyl, tape, CD, I don't even understand what an iPod is. I mostly listen to the radio: jazz, blues, rock, roots, classical, country, hip-hop, soul and anything in-between. Whatever show is on. For some reason listening to my own recordings makes me hyper sensitive to the passage of time. I can listen to a band that Claire and I both liked, then I cry uncontrollably. My music collection is periods of my life.

I almost asked Ms. Violi out. I knew that she'd been on a date because I overheard her telling one of the teachers what a jerk the guy was. I wasn't sure how long you had to wait to ask a woman out, after her spouse has died. It's just a crush. Every time I get the call for the Roberts School I never refuse the work. Call me Nancy, she says, but I call her Ms. Violi. I like in the morning going in to see her to get my class assignment. If I'm lucky, my class's lunch break is at the same time as hers, so I see her in the teacher's lounge. We've even sat together, though often with others at the table. Her husband dropped dead from a aassive heart attack at forty-nine, gone. They were together from high school with three grown children. Last spring I'd made up my mind that I'd ask her out before the end of the school year. If she said no, I'd have all summer to recover face before school starts in the fall. I waited too long.

Never got any calls the last couple of weeks as I expected I might.

The problem with the Roberts School is the lunch lady. Just about the time that I began noticing Ms. Violi, the lunch lady began noticing me. Whenever I turned around, she seemed to be standing there, wiry bleach blond hair, half inch gray brown roots, a mind like an engine with an electric skip. I can be teaching a class on the third floor and for some reason there she is, sticking her head in the door, saying hello, telling me about her trip to the casino in Rhode Island. I walk into the teacher's lounge to get a cup of coffee, I hear the door open and it's her. She mentions how great it would be to have company when she takes the bus tour to look at the fall foliage or watch the Tall Ships come into the harbor. Doesn't everyone deserve a little someone to sit next to if they need it? Unique cult unto themselves, lunch ladies.

AFTER LIVING IN New York and almost moving to L.A., I never thought I'd end up back in Boston. And now Everett: The Jersey of Boston. The cable special I'd done created enough of a stir to generate interest. My agent had auditions, gigs around the country, and promises. Claire and I moved to an apartment in Brooklyn. It wasn't a lush lifestyle. Looking back, considering how much I worked, what came back financially didn't seem to be what I expected. Once or twice I didn't make enough to cover my share of rent. Work slowed. I should have been taking next steps in terms of career, appearances on television shows, my own cable special, but it didn't happen. Eventually my agent dropped me. I picked up another. At first there was a bit more stand-up work, but this dwindled to a trickle. We couldn't afford to live in New York City and resettled in Boston. I don't know where Claire is now.

Yesterday I visited my mother. Skeletal faces looked up from wheelchairs along the hall. They stared, smiled, or looked terrified of me. Others talked at me as if we'd been in an ongoing conversation. One shouted in a language I did't recognize, maybe something Slavic. One woman offered me broken cookies. My mother was in the recreation room: they had children's video running. She sat in a chair staring at the floor. The attendant noticed me and said, look everybody, we have a visitor.

She turned and looked at me blankly. I said hey Ma, let's take a walk. Suddenly she stood up, smiled and said, hey everybody I have a visitor. She walked to me and whispered it's a good thing you came, I've got that, that, what do you call it? I didn't know what she meant. We walked the path that winds around the grounds. It's nice around here she said, I've never been here before, have you? Sometimes I say no. Sometimes I say yes, we walk here whenever

I visit. It doesn't matter what I say. Thirty seconds later it's forgotten.

I took her back inside and we sat on a sofa in the visiting area. She watched the fish. All the love that she gave me and I calculated how soon I could get out. It's not like I had any place to go. While we sat there I overheard one of the attendants relate a story to a fellow worker. She couldn't see us from where she was setting up for lunch service in the dining room. She complained about a certain department store, how recently she'd been shopping there and her three-year old son had to pee. They didn't have a public toilet, so she made him pee on clothes on a rack in the store. When they began serving lunch I walked my mother into the dining room. Each patient is assigned a regular seat. I left her in the hands of the attendant, the one who had her kid piss on the clothes.

LAST NIGHT AS I lay back to finish myself off, Mildred my dental hygienist, appeared in the mix. Mildred's never been on my bench. Other than an on-the-spot-thought when she's doing her cleaning, I'd never given her another thought. This is my team, I'll play and bench anyone I please, but suddenly Mildred appeared in garters and thigh-high stockings, high heels, a corset and began spanking the second grade teacher at the Roberts School, who was going down on me. I went with it. This morning I woke and couldn't focus until I whacked to Mildred again.

There's a man who lives out in the western part of the state who suffered chronic back pain for years. He began praying to a deceased cardinal. Eventually his back pain was cured. Our current cardinal has recently declared this a miracle, and will move to make the deceased cardinal a saint. We can put a man on the moon and do laser surgery. Please come into the 21st century. But the Catholics are in trouble. Many of their flock flew the nest during the current scandal. But hey, God says forgive and forget. What's a few thousand diddled boys? The new Catholic cardinal is a thinking man. What the Catholics need right now is a new saint.

The guy who lives on one side of me is a drunk. Every morning I hear him, a deep, moaning kind of puking, like it hurts all the way. He mostly keeps to himself. Twice there've been fires in his apartment when he's passed out and left something cooking on the stove. But we can't get rid of him because he's the landlord's nephew. Depending on how much he's had, he'll puke late at night too. On the other side is a young woman. I can only assume she has an eating disorder. She builds up slowly. I can tell by the gagging that she's putting her fingers in her throat. Eventually it all comes up. She doesn't seem exceptionally thin. We've chatted a few times in the hall.

Occasionally, I hear her when she's having sex, late at night she arrives home there'll be a man's voice. It doesn't take long and the bed bumping begins. She has a high-pitched yell she lets out during the act. It's a kind of AHHHYAH! AHHHYAH!

NORMAN SAYS that I've mellowed over the years. I certainly don't feel as impulsive as I used to, to prove anyone who disagreed with me an idiot, to shout down opposition, tell off anyone who didn't see things as I did. That's why Claire stopped having me involved when she spent time with her friends, one too many incidents. Nowadays I try, and I sit back, keep my mouth shut. I pretend that I'm open minded, interested in what the person I'm speaking with has to say. Deep down I might be thinking that the person is stupid or a jerk, but no need to let on. That's probably why I mostly keep to myself. I do go out. The apartment is too small and I need to see people. But only long enough to confirm that I really don't like them, that most of the people I run into are stupid, in denial, or both.

In the morning I walk down to the park a few blocks away. I sit on benches and watch the locals gather, seemingly out of nowhere, sharing the first pint, talking about the previous night's brawl, who got a tooth knocked, out who cut her hand. Soon the daycare brigades, row upon row of children holding on to a rope, led by teenage girls who work for the daycare centers, barking out instructions, chasing strays, calming skirmishes. Many of them are Latinas and they speak Spanish with most of the kids. Later I walk to the Italian café, probably the last of a kind. No bullshit American coffee, no comfy-corner laptop folks. The average age of these denizens is seventy-five, the majority from the south of Italy, the last of the big wave of Italian immigrants. There is no English spoken here. There is no Italian spoken here. But a hybrid, broken Italian and broken English, I dare anyone to find a dialect quite like it anywhere else. They yell feverishly at each other, sometimes over Berlusconi's latest tricks, whether ziti or rigatoni is best with meat sauce. Soccer. Their voracious chorale sweeps me back to the sounds of my youth.

Uncle Vinny called Cadillacs Jew Canoes but he drove them. You'll never get anywhere in that racket, he said to me referring to stand-up. He said the kikes have it all wrapped up. Uncle Vinny would badmouth anyone. He badmouthed Italians, even his own friends and family when they weren't around. He and my father once went in on a racehorse. Through an inside connection, they bought a supposedly washed-up horse for cheap, but the catch was the horse could still run. I don't know how much the horse cost, but I know that my mother wasn't happy about it. One night in particular, my mother urged him to reconsider. My father became furious and started screaming at her. He took the living room lamp from the end table and smashed it on the floor. My sister and I were in the kitchen, sitting under the table with our fingers in our ears. The horse couldn't run. My father and Uncle Vinny had been taken, and put the beast down. My uncle swore that kneecaps would be broken.

I ASK MY THERAPIST, is there an end to rage and anger management? Do I have to do this forever? I can stop seeing him if I wish, he says. Maybe it's a good time to take some time off. I still feel rage and anger. Sometimes they get the better of me. I ask my psychiatrist, When does this process end? He asks me how I feel. I say I feel shitty. Why do you feel shitty he wants to know? I don't know. He says that he's been a psychiatrist for almost fifty years, and when someone says they don't know, it means they don't want to do the work to find out. Or maybe they don't want to find out. Or maybe they like feeling shitty. He's blunt, speaks his mind. At eighty years I think he feels there's no time to lose. So he doesn't beat around the bush like my therapist. Why do you come here, he asks? Because if I don't come here you won't give me a prescription for the medication that sometimes helps me feel a little better. How long have you been feeling bad, he asks? I tell him he always asks me that. I've felt bad for as long as I remember.

Then he starts pushing me to where we invariably end up, to that time when I was five or six, and I realized that neither God nor Santa Claus existed. Then he starts in about my father, the loss of trust, and an overwhelming feeling of helplessness. But I felt bad even before that I tell him, maybe as early as three, sitting in a high chair and feeling bad. Things can happen before a person is old enough to walk, he says, things that could have a profound impact on their lives. Then we are out of time. We always pick up, back at the beginning again. With me feeling shitty and him asking me why, and it's the same route until we get to him saying things can happen before a person can walk that can have a profound impact. And then it's time, and I give him my co-payment he asks do I need a prescription, as if he didn't know, and he blindly scribbles one, and when I bring it to the pharmacy they can't read his handwriting. I explain that he is blind, sometime the person behind the counter laughs, as if I'm making a joke. I say no I mean it, he's really blind. It cost me one hundred and ten a month to see my therapist every other week, my shrink once a month, and buy my medication. That's in addition to what I pay each month for health insurance. It's half my rent.

Last Saturday I played an out-of-the way joint on the Cape. Not many tourists, mostly year-round folks, tradesmen and their women, local singles. I opened for a trio that played country covers. I worked cutting my nose into the routine. They liked it. Why not, there I was under the lights with a scab on my nose. The previous day I'd been after a nose hair that taunted me. No matter how many attempts with the clippers, I couldn't quite angle it right. Each time I went for a snip, I would clip and miss and try again. My hand, which normally shakes—I have some kind of tremor—seemed unsuitable to the task. I decided I would make one last attempt. I gripped my right, shaky hand with my left. This helped steady it. I angled my face in the mirror, and snip. I made the commitment and immediately felt the sting of metal through flesh and blood began dropping into the bathroom sink. That drew the best response of the night. I avoided my religious material altogether with that crowd. I kept the show simple and to the point. There were men in the audience willing to fight for what they believe, and me a long way from home.

On the drive back to the city my car broke down. Fortunately, after the eighty-mile drive, the clutch gave out six blocks from my apartment. It was three in the morning, so I managed to park it on the side of the street. The mechanic says it'll be around four hundred dollars. It's an old Toyota with one hundred and sixty thousand miles. Keeping the car is a big expense. I could do my substitute teaching and local gigs without one, but it would be harder to get in and out of town. Norman lent me the money. He said pay him back in September when I start teaching. I said what if something else happens to the car. He says deal with that when the time comes. I used to tell Claire that even if I was sixty, had worked my whole life at it and never made it, I would not regret my choices. Better to do what I wanted, to be free too make the choice.

So now I have a car with a new clutch that still needs extensive work at any time. The mechanic warned that some kind of joint on the driveshaft was on its way out, might get me through fall but if I didn't replace it, it would eventually snap and the driveshaft drop out. I've seen those cars on the side of the road. There are so many myriad things that could go wrong with a car at any given time. The older the car the higher the odds that something will break. This is what I think about on those dark rides home from Hampton Beach or the Cape.

SOME PEOPLE MY AGE are thinking ahead to retirement. I don't know what I would do if I were to retire. I hate golf. I hate Florida. I hate shopping malls, model trains and fishing. I hate those happy old people, what I mean by old is, say, twenty or thirty years older than I am right now. They take long walks, eat out and chew every last bite. Always smiling and saying things like, you're only as old as you feel. They're full of shit. If I work full time as a sub and pick up as many hundred dollar gigs as I have been, I'll be able to pay my rent, car expenses, health insurance, olive oil, pasta and garlic. With a good tail wind I'll have a few extra bucks around if I want to have an espresso, or buy some dark, smelly Italian tuna.

I never fell in with the booze and drug problems like so many folks. Sure, it was all around the scene back in the eighties. But it wasn't just showbiz. Many a carpenter, plumber, cop, or hairstylist had to have their party helmet surgically removed back then. As a teenager I did some drinking and dope smoking. I even tried acid once. I remember thinking how I had cracked the code, found the mystery, looked into the eyes of force that thwarted any human notion of God. I had looked into the heart of creation itself, the universe opened up to me, everything finally made sense. Then I came down and couldn't remember what it was that I had figured out. Back in the early 1970s a lot of downers were around too, as well as speed. Downers put me to sleep. Speed made me more neurotic and intense than I already was. As long as I remember I can take or leave booze. Never liked the hangover, though before medication I was capable of overdoing it, since medication I don't feel the need. Pot helped me relax and sleep, but in the end confused me. I never smoked much. I could buy a small amount and eight months later still have some left. Then it got so expensive, and I got older and it began to make me paranoid. Rather than help me sleep, my mind would race, I'd start thinking of my act, and my life, my mother, and Claire.

Now a couple of drinks are usually my limit. Except for the other night. I won tickets to see some Marx Brothers movies. Norman came along, and afterwards we went out for a drink and it turned in to three or four. I ended up spending the night at Norman's. I cried about what a loser I am and how I had fucked up. Norman listened, tried to be rational, assuring me that I wasn't. If I were a loser, Norman said, he wouldn't be my friend.

I COULD PICK up a local agent. But there's nothing they could do for me that I can't do. I keep up with the various people who book the kinds of places that will have me. Mostly I know them and they know me. There are a couple of real comedy clubs in and around the city where I can still get a mid-week booking each season, but the majority of the work is in the suburbs. Clubs that feature acts like the guitar player from the Electric Prunes. I haven't been to New York or Philly in over a year. Last March I did a gig in Providence. Well, at least I don't have a lot of traveling expenses. Labor Day weekend, I've got a Friday spot at Hampton Beach.

Today temperatures rose to the nineties with high humidity. The old air conditioner pissed and farted trying to keep up. I turned it off and took a drive to Revere Beach. I like the idea of the beach, but I hate it in the end, the salt, sand and stickiness—having to expose my sagging, fleshy body. I parked at the same place my friends and I parked as teenagers. The same place my mother parked when she took me here as a child—across from Bianchi's Pizza, one of the last of the old era. Gone the amusement park, the noisy, creaky old roller coaster, the arcades, the Ferris wheel, dodgem cars and merry-go-round, go-carts, roundup, the whip, cotton candy, hot dogs, clam rolls and French fries. Gone. Replaced by hideous concrete condominiums painted yellow and pink. I sat on the wall for awhile, deciding whether I should spend the money for one of Bianchi's over-sized slices. Mothers with kids were everywhere, women in skimpy bikinis, glazed with oil, lying on beach chairs, old folks, joggers, bikers and bicyclists, I remembered asking my mother for money so my sister and I could go on the rides. She'd give my sister and me fifty cents, and we'd each get two rides out of it. When we got back my mother would have Italian cold cut sandwiches on hand-cut Italian bread. And fruit. After lunch I'd plead with her, could I get a slice of pizza at Bianchi's, and she'd give in.

I walked down close to the water, keeping as much distance from people on chairs and blankets as I could. At one point I took my shoes off. I don't have a bathing suit, but I was wearing a pair of old cut-off dungaree shorts. They were one size too small, and I had to suck in my belly to snap them. At home in the mirror I looked pregnant. Shoes in hand, I stepped gently into the water. To my surprise, it was much warmer than I expected. I had my wallet and cell phone, so I put them in my shoes, then placed them back on shore, looking carefully to see if anyone noticed. I removed my t-shirt and covered my shoes with it. I glanced around to see if anyone could see me, and how bad I looked in my shorts. I wanted to go in for a piss. I pretended to sample the water, splash my arms around. I would have to walk out quite a ways in order to get waist deep. The water, particularly calm, lapped listlessly at the shore. The farther out I walked the more removed from everything I felt. The distance to the shore became distorted. I looked at my clothes and wondered could I reach them in time should someone grab them. Out on the open water I saw a long distance swimmer, arms carving the surface of the water like a machine, the dark outline of a heavy tanker loomed on the horizon, between tanker and swimmer a few sail boats of different sizes gathered up what scant wind could be had. It felt good to piss in the water. I wondered how many men, women and children were pissing in the water up and down the beach at that very moment. I finished, then let my legs out from under me so that I completely submerged myself.

I had no towel so I let the sun dry me. I put my t-shirt on soon as I could then went to sit on the wall watching gulls hover and swoop, and the endless display of people up and down the boulevard. When fully dry, I went to Bianchi's, got a slice, and ate it in the car on the way home. They say the beach makes some people horny. In most cases bathing suits are at least as revealing if not more than underwear. If you walked around downtown Boston in your underwear you might get arrested. At the beach, it's part of the dress code. Later at home I gave it a whack, burping up Bianchi's pizza.

I HAVE A website. But I have no fan base. The last time I checked my site hadn't had a visitor in thirty-one days. Now and again I run across a new booking agent. It's good to refer them to it, so they can make sure I am who I say I am. That I am the guy who did the cable special in the 1980s called *Three Rising Stars* and the other two really did make it to the big time. The photo on the website was taken ten years ago. I'm ten pounds lighter and my hair less gray. I could darken it. Seems like there's no comedians over forty around. They're either on their way up or on their way down. I've seem them come and go. The ones I thought were brilliant that vanished. The ones I thought sucked who made it big. The ones who got the breaks, and the ones who didn't.

Other than Norman, I can't remember the last time I knew anyone in the audience at my gigs. Years ago a few old chums from Medford might show up and harass me. If not for the efforts on Norman's part to maintain a friendship, I might not even have a friend. One thing I can be certain of, whenever I have a show, is that no one in the audience is there to see me.

I recently read an article about how we've evolved as a species to be friend-makers, and how tests have shown that people who don't make friends, usually don't do well in society. Friendship, it's been reported, is part of natural selection. My sister emailed me. She's been thinking of me, and hopes that I am well. Come up for a visit she says. I email her and tell her things are fine. I exaggerate the number of shows I have during the summer. Thanks for the offer, maybe later. After I send the email I realize that she could visit my website any time and see that Thursday night at the Beggar's Pub in Wayland isn't doing okay.

The Three Stooges were my first heroes. From the moment I first saw Moe gouge Larry's eyes, I knew that pain and laughter were the ultimate Yin/Yang. I knew nothing about the Yin and Yang then. In fact I know nothing about it now except it has something to do with opposites being necessary for each other.

Later I discovered the Marx Brothers, Chaplin, Keaton, Woody Allen, Mel Brooks, Monty Python, Firesign Theater. Claire and I spent many evening at the movies. She liked more artsy things. Bergman. She turned me on to Fellini. I've never been able to watch *La Strada* since our split.

Maybe I'm lazy. I don't feel like I can take anything new on. I listen to radio, try to read books and movie reviews, keep abreast of things, but I no longer pursue new musicians, filmmakers, books, comedians the way I did when I was in my twenties and thirties when I had an insatiable appetite for everything. Worse, old favorites simply make me sad about the past, like hearing Sun Ra this morning made me think of Jill, because I took her to see him and she got up and started dancing around with the Arkestra, doing that hippie stomp of hers, making a complete fool of herself.

I seldom use the library any more, except to borrow an occasional movie. In the past I'd spend many an afternoon cooling off in the summer, or kill a couple of hours on a late winter morning, reading through periodicals. One by one they've disappeared with each new budget cut. I especially liked outdoor magazines, fishing and hunting and hiking. When I was a boy I used to buy *Field and Stream* and *Outdoor Life*. I'd fantasize about hunting and fishing and my ultimate dream, to take a horseback trip high into the Rocky Mountains and fish for wild trout.

The closest I ever came were a few Saturday morning hikes to the Medford Woods with the boy scouts. Reading those magazines in the library all these years later, it struck me how nothing has changed. Oh, the writers had changed but the stories were the same. Who shot the new world record elk with a bow. The ten best trout fishing rivers in North America. Catch largemouth bass during those lazy, hazy days of summer. And then there are near tragedy stories: how I survived six days lost in the Everglades, how I survived shooting myself in the foot and hopping thirty miles through the wildernes.

TODAY AS I WALKED home from the café a woman approached me. Excuse me she said, do you have a moment? Caught off guard, and sensing she might need some kind of assistance, I said I did. Everything happened so quickly by the time I had those words out of my mouth, I saw the pamphlets and realized she was ready to give me some kind of God pitch. I said, look, I really have no time or interest, and proceeded to walk away, but she persisted and followed. Have you ever thought about heaven she asked? I turned. I've already asked you to leave me alone. She was maybe ten years younger than me, dark complexion, perhaps Hispanic though she spoke perfect English. She wore a knee-length tan skirt and a colorful sleeveless top, a pair of hoop earrings and a smile.

I took note of her round hips and fit arms. I surmised she'd birthed a couple of children though she had no ring on. I've been around a long time I told her, and have been thinking about these things for a long time too, and with all due respect, I didn't go around and try to convert others to my way of thinking, and don't appreciate strangers approaching me on the street to do the same. My name is Teresa she said. I'm not a stranger now. That's not what I mean, I said. Don't you ever wonder what heaven must be like she asked? No I haven't I answered, not since 1962.

By now my attraction to her had won over my anger. If not, I would have told her to take her God and stick it where the candles don't shine. A moment passed and she looked me in the eye. She asked me what's my favorite thing to do. I told her I didn't know. You must have something you really like to do she said, everyone does. Do you like the Red Sox? No I said, in fact I hate the Red Sox. How can you hate the Red Sox and be from Boston she wanted to know. Then she asked me where's my favorite place and I told her I didn't have one. You must have some place that is special to you she said. Where do you live she asked, and I told her down the street. Well pretend it's your favorite place and that you love it. Then she inquired about my favorite food and I told her my mother's Sunday dinner. Okay, okay she said excitedly, as if she'd scored one. Imagine you get to spend eternity in your own house eating your mother's Sunday dinner forever and forever—that's heaven. I asked her where she got her information. She said it's all in the Bible, and God wrote the Bible so it can't be wrong. It broke my heart that someone so cute and shapely could be so stupid and unimaginative. Furthermore, as much as I loved my mother's Sunday dinner, I wouldn't want to spend eternity eating nothing but macaroni, meatballs and braciole. And now that the air conditioner finally broke, if I were to die, my apartment was no place to spend forever.

IN ADDITION TO gambling my father loved gardening. He took pride in his tomatoes and other vegetables. One day every spring a neighbor would come around announcing the manure truck was on its way. My father would put the word out to stop at our house, purchase several dozen baskets and dump it on the newly turned soil of his garden. Since everyone else in on our street did the same, the neighborhood smelled for days. To make matters worse, my father made a special brew, by combining water and manure in a fifty-gallon drum, allowing it to ferment, keeping an ever-watchful eye over it. I remember him coming home from work and watching over the barrel, a cigarette hanging out his mouth, stirring its contents with a long stick. Over the next weeks he would scoop it up with buckets and pour it over certain plants.

My Uncle Vinny used to say always check the rearview mirror. I think it had to do with a woman's ass. He also said that if there's one thing worse than the Irish it's the Boston Irish. Uncle Vinny never went in for gardening. If the horses weren't running he chased the dogs, or a card game. My uncle was different from my father. If he hit at the track or at cards, he'd come home with a happy booze glow and a bag full of Chinese takeout. Pick out a toy he'd say to us if we were out at a store. If my father won, it never showed in his personality, and he kept the money to himself. I liked my Uncle Vinny. At the time I really thought he got hurt on the job and that's why he didn't work. He let me swear. I was sad when he, my aunt and cousins moved out of the apartment on the second floor. He did a great imitation of Woody Woodpecker. I don't understand why I still think of this these decades later. Like I can still smell the neighborhood after the manure truck passed through, hear my uncle's voice doing Woody Woodpecker, fight with my cousin over the last Chinese spare rib.

It's too hot to sleep. I priced fans today and determined that the summer is half over and I can't afford one. There's a party in the neighborhood, I can hear Latin music and smell grilling meat. About an hour ago, the girl next door came home and within minutes had a half hour sex session now everything is quiet. It's Saturday night. Norman met a woman and they are out on their first date. Who else is alone tonight? Even my mother shares a room.

I TRY TO TRACE it back to a time when she didn't forget things, or insist that she were right about something when she wasn't. Uncle Vinny always called her ditsy. He made fun of my mother. She often said oh I didn't know that. Uncle Vinny mocked her and said oh I didn't know that. It became a catch phrase around the family. If we drove outside the city without my father she frequently got lost. One time we went to visit an aunt who had moved to a new house on the South Shore, even with directions she got lost. I cried. She pretended for a long time. And worked hard not to let on. One night I visited her and she was making spinach and baby meatball soup. She brought the soup to the table there were no baby meatballs. I asked her Ma, where's the baby meatballs and when she realized she forgot to make them she cried.

I've got all the windows open but there's no air moving. I lie in bed naked over a sweaty sheet. Always I hear Spanish music, and smell grilled meat. I'm hungry, but all I have is tuna fish. I had the cable turned off because I can't afford it. I usually spent my time channel surfing, sometimes hours at a time if I couldn't sleep. Years back, before medication the sleepless nights meant hours of racing thoughts and near hysteria. Now, the sleepless periods are shorter, less frequent, and not nearly as intense. I worry about my mother, my sister who I haven't seen in over a year, about gigs and things I wished I'd never said, and Claire, how I insulted her sister at a Thanksgiving dinner in front of her family. I worry about what will happen if I get seriously ill, or how I am going to come up with the insurance payment on the car. I think about the rider less horse in Fellini's *La Strada*, sometimes obsessively. I think about kids I hung out with when I was a teenager, I see and hear them in my mind as if yesterday were now. Eventually I fall asleep.

I never was part of a hip young comic circle. Oh they were around, and got attention. Some folks went on to big things. I came in the back door. I never acted, never went to one of the spawning colleges like Emerson. Five years of open mics. Eventually I began getting open mic features, and they paid. These days I take any open mic feature that I can. Who am I to refuse the work?

I TIMED MY drive to Milky's in Leominster to coordinate with the open mic. I wanted to arrive some time around the end so I wouldn't' have to sit through it. Leomintser is far enough out that I could easily lie about getting stuck in traffic, or say there was an accident on the highway, so not to insult anyone of the open mic performers, or Milky. The air had cooled and dried out in the last few days. Once past the Concord Rotary, the smell of fresh cut hay held sway. The traffic lessened and Route 2 opened out ahead of me. I listened to a cassette tape of Lenny Bruce. The tape deck in my apartment had broken years ago and I never replaced it. I kept a portable recorder for rehearsing otherwise my car remained the last refuge for the tired, dying loops. Bruce's bit about how it's hard to figure out the difference between a piece of art with a little shit in the middle or a piece of shit with a little art in the middle. The tape began to hiss and slowly seized.

The doorman said five bucks. I told him who I was, he said, sorry, go on in where I met Milky who worked the bar and owned the place. A short, stocky man in his fifties, his bald head shone, but he let the wiry, gray and white stuff grow long on the sides and back, and he wore a Jerry Garcia t-shirt. You get two beers and dinner he said, pointing me to an empty seat at the bar. The open mic will be over shortly, we'll take a break before you go on. You want to eat now he asked? Fine with me. In addition to food and drink, I also got half of the door take. Sometimes these kinds of things can work out fine, as there's never a shortage of people who will pay to perform in front of an audience. Dinner turned out to be a cup of chowder that tasted canned, and a burger and fries. Hungry, I made quick work of it. I had a light beer on tap. It tasted like sour water. Milky asked would I like another and I opted for a glass of seltzer.

The open mic continued and I tried to pay a little attention to the waif-like, tattooed and pierced youngster named Star, who rambled on about what women really want in a man vs. what men think women really want in a man. The man who went on last looked like a retiree from the local furniture factory, his jokes were typed and he read them. They were right out of the *Farmer's Almanac*.

I went for the lowest common denominator: the differences between men and women. I wanted to show that smarmy little urchin how to handle such material, but she was busy chatting it up with some pseudo-hipster at the bar, and neither of them paid attention to me. I moved on to sex and my list of things that can go wrong during anal sex. I got a few laughs, a few grunts of disapproval. I did my bit about Christian rock and what could be more antithetical to the spirit of rock and roll? Imagine what a loser you must be if you aspire to be a Christian rock star? Why would anyone want to do it without the sex and drugs? I did my list of Christian rock songs and songwriters like "Everybody Must Get Stoned" by Saint Stephen, "Fire" by Saint Joan of Arc or "I'm A Backdoor Man" by Saint Gets-Moved-Around-A-Lot.

Half of the open mic folks had left before I started. A few of the ones who remained came up to me afterwards and said they enjoyed my act. I made excuses, like the long drive back to Boston, so that I wouldn't get stuck hanging around and talking with anyone in case it might be expected. Milky handed me some cash as I made to leave. I put it in my pocket and shook his hand. Come out again he said. I told him I would. When I got to my car I took the money out. Sixty-five dollars. A near full moon sat low in the sky and followed me back down Route 2. I listened to a tape of Beatles outtakes, and sang along like some silly Baby Boomer confusing nostalgia with significance. For a few moments I actually felt good, or at least I thought so. I began to think about things that could go wrong with the car, and didn't shake it until the Boston skyline came into view.

NORMAN IS dating again. He never learns. After all the failed marriages and relationships he still picks up and starts over. He likes the company, even though in theory, he believes that all relationships are doomed. His new girlfriend has a friend and they want to fix us up. I tell Norman this isn't high school and the last thing I need is a relationship. I have no money. I live in dumpy apartment. I have no future. I'm fine when you first get to know me but as a partner I'm overbearing, controlling, opinionated, vindictive, and a bully. That's what Claire said. She lived with me longer than anyone so she must know. But I've changed since then Norman points out. I'm not the person I was ten or twenty years ago. True, but I see myself as a street fighter, who was later taught to box and move. That's all well and good in the early stages of the fight, but the first time he gets tagged good, he reverts to his old street fighting ways. Knowing is not the same as doing.

Norman suggests that we have a simple get together. No blind date. I give in. He is right. What else have I got to do? I will cook one of my mother's Sunday dinners, on Sunday afternoon, at his condo in Somerville. Norman pays for the groceries and I arrive with them at his place around eleven. It's been years since I've cooked one of my mother's sauces from scratch. I start with good canned tomatoes, fresh basil, and some tomato paste. I sauté garlic and some pancetta in a big sauce pan then add the tomatoes, basil, paste, salt and pepper. I mix up a batch of meatballs, and make a beef braciole. I add them to the sauce and simmer it down for about two hours. I've got imported rigatoni for the pasta course and for an appetizer I fix sautéed breaded artichoke hearts with a squeeze of lemon on the side. The women arrive and rave about the aroma.

I meet Norman's new friend and do the heard-a lot-about-you routine. Then I'm introduced to Char-lene, as attractive as Norman said with her bouncy red hair and full figure, a face the map of Ireland. According to Norman she's only a few years younger than me, though she appears to be ten years my junior. My first reaction is why would anyone who looks like that be interested in me? We shake off the introduction jitters with a couple of glasses of wine. Norman does most of the talking. Norman loves to talk, his girlfriend Sonia appears delighted with him, and once or twice I sneak a glance at Charlene to see that she is as cute as I think. At one point I catch her sizing me up. By three we're on our third bottle of wine and enjoying the food. Charlene asks me where I learned how to cook and I talk about my mother, and being in the kitchen with her on Sunday mornings, certain I must be scoring points.

We sit for a long time after lunch, chatting, getting to know each other the way people who meet for the first time do. Norman suggests that we take the T into the North End for coffee and dessert. Great idea I say along with the others, though secretly, I don't mean it. By now I'm tiring, anxious, wanting to go home. Nonetheless we press on to the North End. After espresso, anisette and dessert in one of the old cafés, we walk down some back streets. Suddenly I find myself walking next to Charlene, Norman and Sonia behind us enough to insure privacy. I don't know what to say. That really was a memorable meal she says breaking the silence. I guess I have to thank my mother I respond. I can't believe I brought my mother up at a time like this. I stop and point to a building. My grandparents lived there I tell her. But it's not the building that they lived in. Then I go into a rant about how this used to be a real neighborhood, and now it's just a gentrified tourist trap. I'm waving my hands around, fuming about restaurants that used to be a grocery or drug store. That trattoria was Anna's Market I exclaim. I used to buy slush there I shout. She looks at me questioningly, and I think I must be coming on too strong. I change the subject and ask her to tell me more about her work. She troubleshoots software. I'm half listening, wondering why she's never been married, angry at Norman and Sonia for setting Charlene and me up to be walking alone. At one point we're so close our hands, hanging by our sides, touch. I move mine away.

I SPENT MOST of yesterday sitting around my apartment, unable to focus. My mind kept turning from my mother, to my work, to Charlene. Norman phoned in the morning to say that Sonia told him that Charlene liked me and I should call her. I tried working on my upcoming routine at Hampton Beach, but couldn't keep my mind on it. I checked my emails to find nothing but ads and sex come-ons. I tried reading but couldn't make it through a paragraph. I knew that I might never have the chance to date a woman as young and attractive as Charlene again. She was smart, and independent. But what would we do? Where would we go after those first few dates? How could I possibly undress in front of her with my sagging flesh, and the skin-growth inside my upper thigh near my scrotum? What if I couldn't perform? What if we fell in love? What if we wanted to live together? We couldn't live in my tiny apartment. She owned a condominium, would she let me move in? And what about when all the veneer wore off, and she began to see me for the person I really am, and vice versa? It was all too much.

Early in the afternoon the guy next door puked. I took comfort in the fact that he too was alone, sitting in his apartment, and in worse shape than me. I tried to whack off, imagining Charlene and her marvelous breasts, but couldn't get a rise, which is often the case with someone new. I brought in some regulars from the bench but only made it to half-mast. Norman had been taking Viagra, speaking its wonders. But Norman had an active sex life and I knew that the last thing I needed was to sit around alone with a hard dick. I felt tired and tried to nap unsuccessfully. I counted down the days to the beginning of the school year, and the first paycheck, provided I got work right away. Around mid-afternoon heavy thunderstorms moved through the area leaving cooler, drier air behind. I decided to walk to the café for an espresso. The men were all arguing, loudly, about Berlusconi's latest scandal. Seems he'd taken up with a teenage girl. It's good to be the Italian prime minister.

On my way home I stopped at the park and sat on a bench. Plump young mothers spoke to each other in Spanish and periodically barked out at their children playing on the swings and monkey bars. A musical ice cream truck pulled up and the kids charged off to it,

At home I ate leftover meatballs and macaroni I had taken from Norman's. I watched the local news at six. Eunice Kennedy died and all three of the stations were running with the story for all it was worth. As Kennedy's go, she seems to have been the real hero of the clan. The Kennedy family made a statement, something to the effect that it was hard to imagine her gone, but now she was with her dead siblings and parents in heaven. I wondered what kind of heaven might accept a bootlegger, or a married president who fucked women in the oval office of the White House. Maybe there was hope for a creep like me, and heaven meant sold out audiences coast to coast who thought I was the greatest thing since the hula-hoop. Maybe my father was there, and heaven for him was hitting an eternal trifecta. Before my mother hit obvlion, her final frontier, she used to say all she wanted to do was die and go to heaven. Around eight o'clock in the evening the girl next door arrived home, gagged herself, then puked.

I WON TICKETS to the new Woody Allen movie and decided I would call Charlene. Each time I made a move to phone her I talked myself out of it, and never saw the movie. I've grown tired of Allen's movies, centered in his self-absorbed neurosis and love affairs with young women. But someone capable of his early classics might surely, at some point, make a comeback.

I felt helpless. Four days in a row I'd been moping around the apartment, feeling bad for myself. I had a therapy appointment and cancelled it with the excuse that I had an upset stomach. I called early, before he's in his office, and left a message. Later in the morning my phone rang. He was calling to reschedule but I didn't pick up. There were two more calls during the day. When I checked in the evening, there were two messages from my therapist, a third from my sister. She'd be coming to town next week could she take me out to lunch. I phoned her back and we chatted. Her daughter was off to Columbia this fall. Her son was going into his senior year at high school, captain of the baseball team. She and her husband were planning a trip to Europe. I had nothing to say. Good. Oh that sounds terrific. Wow, Europe. While we spoke there were police sirens outside. I looked out the window. Cops had some guy handcuffed, and sitting on the sidewalk. A woman waved her hands, shouting frantically in Spanish at a policeman.

It was Wednesday afternoon and one of my favorite rock and roll shows aired. Gorilla Got Me: rejects, rebels, and assorted losers. It amounted to garage rock from the 1950s to the present—the songs that never made the charts, nor got close. Alas, if only there were such a venue for comedians. Half an hour into the show I turned it off. I couldn't get enthused. When I heard Johnny Thunders' "Born to Lose", I remembered the time that Claire and I had seen him at the old Jonathan Swifts in Cambridge. He tried to insight a riot by encouraging the audience to turn their tables upside down. The manager pulled the plug on him. Claire never liked my garage rock tastes. She liked rock, but for her, polish and production had to be evident. We argued all the way home, I thought it was Johnny at his best, and she thought he had no right to take people's money.

I made some spaghetti with garlic and olive oil, and ate. Then I decided to take a walk. The humidity had returned, you could hear a collective drone of air conditioners their discharge water dripped down and made puddles on the ground. I passed a three-family with a statue of the Virgin Mary out front. Could she really get pregnant without having sex? Sounds like a story my father would tell.

I MET MY SISTER at a sandwich shop near the nursing home. Without her I don't know what would have become of my mother. I could never repay her for all the time she put in over the years: the doctor appointments, handling legal and monetary affairs. She took many a day out of her busy schedule to drive down from Vermont and meet my mother's needs. Slowly it became too much until we both knew that my mother would be better off in the home, getting the full time care she needed. For a brief time my sister took my mother in with her in Vermont. It was like having a toddler around for Anna. Several times my mother wandered away from the yard and into the woods that surround Anna's house. It was a set-up for disaster.

They'd walked that morning, and my mother confused Anna with her older sister, my Aunt Rose, dead for years. No matter how hard Anna tried to explain, my mother continued to call her Rose and refer to things from her childhood. Anna and I laughed about the time when we were kids, I was five or six and Anna a year younger. My father had been gambling heavily, and there'd been lots of fighting in the house. My mother phoned a priest from our local parish to come and speak with my father. He became outraged that my mother would tell private business to the priest. After the priest left my parents had an argument. That usually meant my mother trying to speak in a rational tone, my father screaming and breaking things. Anna and I decided that we would run away from home. The very next morning we rose before our parents and left. We walked around the neighborhood for what seemed to be hours, but in reality couldn't have been more than thirty minutes. When we arrived home, hungry for breakfast, our parents were still sleeping and never learned of our adventure.

I got uneasy when Anna asked how things were going for me. Had I been seeing anyone? I explained about Charlene. Anna said that I wasn't getting any younger, and growing old alone didn't have much to commend it. I offered my usual excuses about how difficult it was to meet people, and at my age I no longer felt that a permanent relationship suited me. There are worse things than growing old alone I said. Like what she asked? Like dying young I told her. She said that she and her husband were going to the Maine Shore on Labor Day Weekend. They were thinking of driving down to Hampton Beach to catch my show. I told her not to waste her time I wished that they wouldn't.

She wondered why I wouldn't spend the night. It's easier for me I explained. I never sleep well if I'm away, especially after a show as I'm so hyped up. The drive back helps to unwind. She saw through my lie and knew I didn't make enough to warrant a hotel. After lunch Anna wrote me out the monthly check for my mother's expenses. There's a little something extra she said, folding the check and sliding it across the table to me. Get yourself a room on Labor Day, and get out of town for a couple of days, it will do you good. I put the check in my shirt pocket. In the parking lot we hugged goodbye. Say hello to Fred and the kids I said. I love you she told me. I told her I loved her too.

So here I am. Fifty-four years old today. Moping around my apartment. In the morning I have a piece of toast. Lunchtime I eat another piece of toast. Anna gave me five hundred dollars. That's three times what she usually gives me for my mother's needs. I could take myself out for dinner, and there I'd be, a cliché at table forty-five, where they put the singles and losers. I could let it slip to my waiter that it's my birthday, and get a free dessert with a sparkler.

My sister phones at two but I don't pick up. She leaves me a message, happy birthday hope you're having a good day. At two I switch on Research and Development playing avant-garde and forward-looking jazz, as the DJ likes to call it. I suddenly get the urge for some cold beer, and run to the store around the corner to buy a six-pack. I sit back with a glass of beer, listening to the music. Today in the classic tenor corner it's Joe Lovano, I saw him the first time with Claire. We were in New York and wandered into a little supper club in the Village. And there, Joe blew, with a marvelous sextet while Claire and I dined on Spanish food. By the time the DJ says he'll see us next week, I'm feeling the beers on little food. I turn off the electro-techno program that's beginning.

I decide to take a walk, first the park where some teenagers who work for a local daycare line up toddlers holding onto a rope. Two young men kick a soccer ball to each other on the basketball court. Three young teenage girls stop to smoke, and eye the two men kicking the soccer ball. The girls wear shorts, so short they're cut off at the crotch, and what look to be bikini tops. They can't be older than fourteen. At the café I order an espresso and look at an Italian newspaper, though I can only read a few words here and there. There's a picture of Berlusconi on the front page the headline says something like, Berlusconi tells the opposition to go fuck itself. Now there's a man who knows the importance of a high public profile. Any exposure is good exposure. If I had Facebook I could look up Claire. Maybe she got divorced, I could phone her, and by some miraculous shot of Cupid we'd get back together again. I finish my espresso and drink a glass of water. I feel steadier now. I could walk to Little Tony's and treat myself. It's an old dive that makes a decent red sauce.

Instead I return home. On the way I stop at the store and splurge on a can of dark Italian tuna. I cook spaghetti with garlic, olive oil and tuna. I don't want to stay in Hampton Beach. But if my sister finds out that I didn't, it'll be embarrassing since she gave me the money. What could be worse than being alone in a Hampton Beach motel? Anna certainly won't be in a Hampton Beach motel. I'm sure she'll be in a quaint bed and breakfast, located on a cove with a name you can carve into wood. Why not? Anna's worked hard, so has her husband. They're good people. But the last thing I want to see, is the two of them in the audience at The Wharf.

THIS MORNING I visited my mother. Hurricane Dennis is a hundred or so miles off shore and soaking the coast. I brought her a box of chocolate cherries, it being too wet to take her out to lunch. When I arrived I found her dancing with the recreation woman, to the tune of an old cha-cha, counting out the beat, perfectly, one two cha-cha-cha, as graceful as forty years ago when she and my father would dance at one of their back yard cookouts, or a wedding, or the anniversary party for Uncle Vinny and Aunt Angie. The only thing I knew my parents to enjoy together was dancing. Fast or slow, they cut lovely carpet. The recreation woman tells me that she has a hard time keeping up with my mother, who still remembers steps to all her old dances.

The nurse administering medications told my mother that her son was here pointing my way. My mother turned and looked at me. A strained expression came over her face. That's my son, she asked, the nurse. Then her face changed to a smile. I know

104

you, she said. Come dance with me. I couldn't say no. This is my son, she boasted to those who were still awake, strewn around the room in chairs and wheelchairs, as she tried to show me the steps. Some watched, the nurse, the recreation woman, the few women, and fewer men, who glared or smiled or drooled.

We walked to the visiting area and sat on a sofa looking at tropical fish swim around in a big oblong tank. In a chair against the wall, a shriveled woman sat holding her walker in front of her. It bore a homemade license plate that read Jean. The plate was attached to a basket, full of handkerchiefs that she continually pulled out and fidgeted with, all the while smiling. I looked over my mother's shoulder at the clock, checking how much time before lunch, when I could leave her in the dining room. A man rolled up to us in a wheelchair and said hello to my mother, calling her by her name. She said hello then made to introduce me, but forgot who I was. I introduced myself as her son and she said, oh yes, this is my son. The man rolled away. She looked at me and asked, Where were you born?

I left her at her usual spot in the dining room, as they were serving up Salisbury steak. On the way home the rain came down so hard I had to pull over on the Revere Beach Parkway. I waited five or ten minutes, until it let up enough to drive the rest of the way. At home I made some notes for my Hampton

Beach gig. I had nothing lined up after Labor Day weekend. In town July and August were slow, and now was the time to be hitting up the clubs for fall work. I didn't have the will to turn the computer on and get started. If I don't I'll have no work. Maybe it's time to get out. Many artists do. I've read of painters, poets, musicians, who at some point in their lives, they just hung it up. They know that they've done what they set out to do and taken it as far as they can. There's nothing undignified about that.

MY SISTER ANNA wanted to meet for dinner at a restaurant in Portsmouth. I told her that I usually don't like to eat before a show. She insisted, how often did we have the chance to spend some time together? I drove up to Hampton Beach and tried several motels but they were booked. I worked my way down the strip to The Moulten, under new management, and working hard to make my stay at Hampton Beach enjoyable. They had one or two rooms left, the woman said, but no singles. I took a double. Inside my room I checked the bedding and it looked to have been changed. On the walls hung dusty prints of cottages nestled beside the sea, with boats in the background. I examined the empty closet then hung up my slacks and shirt. Everything else I kept in my bag.

I had a couple of hours to kill and decided to take a walk, but the closer I got to the center of town, the energy of the Masses out for one last summer hurrah scared me. I could smell fried food, hear cries of the crowd and sounds of the arcade. I made an about-face, walking the opposite direction along a sidewalk that followed the coast, past rows of old beach cottages and the occasional new condominium complex. Most of the places were full of people, out on balconies, porches and roofs, drinking beer and listening to music or the baseball game. The sun had been in and out all day, temperatures were in the low 70s, but a few braved a dip in the ocean. Here and there a couple of young women with perfect bodies that only a twenty-one year old could have, walked past wearing bikinis.

I decided that I would pay for dinner even though it would set my finances way back. I knew that Anna would insist, but I was long overdue. Anna had been good to me. She got a lot from my mother, honest and hardworking. Hard to believe she became a stockbroker. I hadn't seen her husband Fred in five years. He'd aged, gained a few pounds, but who hadn't? Fred and I went way back. We were in rival gangs in Medford. He hung out at Playstead Park. My hangout was in front of the Spring Street Spa. I tried to avoid fighting, never had the stomach for it. One particular brawl between our gangs, a friend of mine named Wolf bit the nose off a friend of Fred's known as Hawk. Wolf later said that he would always remember the sensation of the Hawk's nose bones, crunching in his teeth. Fred and I never fail to joke about the incident, and this dinner no different. Fred said last he'd heard, the Hawk had retired from the post office. Wolf was an early AIDS victim.

Anna met Fred right after high school. Fred was digging ditches for Di Marco Construction at the time. Thirty years later he's got his own construction thing going, and done quite well for a kid from the streets of Medford. Anna loved him from the start and they never looked back. We talked a little of the old days, and Anna and Fred's kids. Fred and Anna are going to Europe in the fall, and they shared their itinerary with me. We talked a little about my mother. Anna asked did I ever call Charlene back. I answered with a playful, oh you never know. I ate a green salad, broiled blue fish and drank one glass of white wine. Anna and Fred had appetizers, dinner, second glasses of wine and dessert. I held off to keep the check as low as possible. On my way in I'd given my debit card to the hostess to make sure my sister didn't scoop the check out from under me. When I asked the waiter for the check, he brought my card back and told me it had been taken care of. I know your tricks Anna said. She'd phoned ahead that afternoon.

The room was noisy during my act, but the place was full. I used the vision of the Virgin Mary bit, citing the most recent case in point: a smudge on a window at a local hospital that some people claim is the face of the Virgin Mary. Hundreds and hundreds of people, adults and children, have been gathering around, pointing and praying and taking pictures. The local news interviewed them on television, she's the mother of God one of them said, I believe in God so I had to come and see her for myself.

In Italy there's a mountain on top of which stands the Cathedral of the Virgin Mary. An unpaved road winds up the mountain and all along the way people, mostly Italian women, old and hunched over, walk up barefoot as an offering to the Virgin Mary. Their nylons and stockings are torn underfoot. Their feet become scraped, cut and bruised. They visit the cathedral to pray, and on the way down, they hold their breath and get lashed by village virgins wielding thorny branches. My first girlfriend Tina Zamboni had a cousin born unable to walk so she spent her childhood in a wheelchair. I asked Tina if God exists, why would he do that? Tina said people like her cousin were God's angels. Tina could jerk me off with either hand.

Only when the lights raised did anyone notice I'd left. I heard a few polite claps. The place erupted when the twins took the stage: Kim and Brooke, high-heels, blond-hair, mini-dresses and implants with big cleavage. They told jokes about their mother's womb, and switching around with guys they dated. Kim, I think it was Kim it could have been Brooke, played the dumb one and Brooke, it could have been Kim, played the smart one. Maybe smart, maybe not. My guess is that they have a future in this business, as long as their faces and tits hold up.

I went on too long with the religion stuff and forgot to do the bit about not understanding how to use my cell phone. I can dial out and retrieve messages, nothing more. I have no idea what texting is. I don't know what a BlackBerry is. It used to be a fruit. I call a repairman if my coffee machine doesn't work. I think there's a time in anyone's life when you reach the point where you can't take on anymore, especially in terms of technology. You have to put your foot down and say not one more thing.

Anna and Fred left about half way through the Cutesy Twins. They had a ways to drive back up to their inn. Anna said she loved the show, and gave me a warm hug. Fred said good to see you, and gave me the kind of handshake that only someone working with his hands for thirty-five years can give. I stayed to the end of the twins' act. Then I returned to my room. I removed my shoes, sat on the edge of the bed, and looked around. From the room on one side of me I could hear The Who's "We Won't Get Fooled Again", and a couple of guys singing along with no concern for timing or key. On the other side I could hear voices of a man and woman. They seemed to be arguing. I got up from the bed and went to the wall for a closer listen. She was sobbing, slurring her words but repeating, you do this every fucking time

Timmy, every fucking time. Timmy would respond with one or two words, but in a lower register so I couldn't make them out. I put my on my shoes, zipped up my bag, went out to my car and drove home.

I PHONED THE school department and told them I was available to work full time. I owed Norman money, the first heating bill would be in soon, and the last car insurance payment was due. After twenty-one worked days in a row, the rate for substitute teachers climbs twenty-five dollars a day. I never got that far. Besides, I heard from other subs that when you get that close, they don't call you one day so that you have to start over again. Occasionally there are emergencies when a teacher might be out for a long time, if you're lucky enough to get that class for the duration, it could pay off. The longest I ever taught the same class was two or three days. The woman I spoke with said it would likely be slow for a couple of weeks, but on teacher training days I might hear from them. Teacher training days are when the teacher goes for some kind of training, and the city pays a substitute to teach their class.

I sent about two-dozen emails to area clubs. To the booking agents I didn't know I introduced myself. To those I already knew, I said hello and politely asked for a night some time over the next couple of months. I heard right back from Jeff Hartly. Jeff's been running the open mic on Tuesdays at the Cantab in Central Square, Cambridge, for thirty years. It's one of the better-respected open mic features. Jeff draws a regular crowd and there's always an array of newcomers, all wanting to break you up. Jeff splits the gate with the feature and it can mean a good night's pay. His email read, booked through November, get back in touch I can hook you up in December.

Today Norman and I met at the café. He was on his way up to the Lynn District Court for a case. He asked how my finances were. I told him I might make it. Don't worry about the money I lent you for the car he said. When I have it, give it to him. Then he said that he had something to tell me. It seems my old girlfriend Jill, the butcher, had been trying get in touch with me. Norman had recently lunched with his third wife, or had dinner with his second wife, but one of them knew Jill. It was his third wife because she and Jill got to know each other when she and Norman were married, and Jill and I were living together. It seems that Jill had contacted Norman's wife on Facebook inquiring about my whereabouts and status. She'd tried looking me up on Facebook but found nothing. That's exactly why I don't want to be on Facebook, I told Norman. So that I don't have to be tracked down by all these faces from the past, each wanting to catch up. Norman agreed.

But my curiosity got the best of me. I broke. I asked Norman, what did she say? Did Susan, Norman's third wife, tell her anything? Where is she, what's she doing, did she say anything to Susan? I don't want her to know anything about me I claimed. Norman said that all he knew was that she had contacted Susan on Facebook. I always liked her Norman said. You like all women I said to Norman. He agreed. You didn't like her because she didn't shave. That's not true I said. That never bothered me. After awhile I just got used to it. It's true that Jill didn't shave her legs or under her arms. She was the first woman I ever was intimate with who didn't. Uncomfortable with the idea at first, it quickly became normal to me. She had nice tits, Norman said. She did, I replied.

By the end of the week I heard back from about a dozen of my inquiries. Most of them said they were booked through November, try back in a month or so, they might be able to give me something over the winter. A few of them said that the clubs were no longer doing comedy. Two were bounced back no longer valid addresses. I could feel the change in the season. The days were shorter and cooler. In the morning I had to close the window. This year I would hold out turning the heat on, and even when I did, it would be sparingly. I went into my dresser and assessed my fall and winter wear. I hadn't bought any new clothes in two or three years. My sweaters were worn and stretched, my shirts frayed and colors faded. I had one pair of wool black slacks and one pair of brown corduroys. Both pairs of paints were now a full size too small around the waist. My underwear and socks were thin.

I HEARD BACK from a club down in Bridgewater. I took a chance as it's a new place, and I sent my inquiry off blindly. Sandy Bennett booked for Tim's Tavern. On Thursday nights they had comedy before Karaoke. Her boss Tim said he knew of me. They paid a hundred flat fee and dinner. She offered several dates in October. I chose one. Even if I had four or five gigs like that a week it would be hard to survive.

I thought about Jill. I could get her email address, or phone number, from Norman's ex-wife. Maybe she wants to get back together. Last time we had any contact she'd taken up with an acupuncturist and healer. They'd been living together for about six months. Anything could have happened between then and now. Maybe she's given up the New Age stuff and is an atheist. With my luck she'd be a Libertarian. Better to sit around and lament about the past. What I did wrong. What I could or couldn't change about myself. In therapy I learned that you just become addicted to being sad, or angry about things like divorce or religion or a parent.

My therapist phoned later in the morning. Between his annual August vacation, and my skipping a meeting, I hadn't been to see him in nearly a month. I made an appointment for as far away as he'd allow. Funny how when my therapist or psychiatrist get me on the phone, even though they're both blind, it's like they can see right through me. They know that I'm trying to avoid them, tired of the same old talk, month after month, year after year. My therapist says I've made lots of progress in our ten years together. My psychiatrist wants me to tell him about my worst nightmares.

My Uncle Vinny used to say never trust a doctor. After he had himself brained by a shovel, he never went to the doctor except when he had the lung cancer that killed him. The priest delivered a eulogy, and in true Catholic tradition, it had nothing to do with the deceased. Uncle Vinny certainly had a place in heaven, the priest assured us all. My uncle spent the better part of his adult life collecting crooked disability, gambling, chasing women, and in the later years, sitting back in a recliner watching *The Beverly Hillbillies* reruns in a cloud of cigarette smoke.

I never knew my grandfather. He died in World War II. I've heard mixed stories of what happened. One that my mother tells is he died when his village was bombed. She never knew if it was the Americans or the Germans who bombed the village. My Uncle Vinny always said that Grandpa died protecting the people he loved. My father remained silent on the matter. My mother always said if you knew my grandmother, you'd know why Uncle Vinny and my father turned out the way they did. She died when I was only ten. My father and Uncle Vinny finally sent for her, after putting it off for many years. She never forgave them. But she was a witch according to my mother, an evil person. And my mother rarely said such things about anyone. The only reason my father and Uncle Vinny finally brought her from Italy was because she bribed them. Whatever she'd been doing in Italy, she aMassed a little bit of money, and my father and uncle couldn't resist the ultimate payday, playing odds that at her age, she wouldn't be around much longer. I only knew an old woman for a few years. She fawned over me in a language I couldn't understand. I heard that when she finally left Italy, the people in the village had a celebration thanking the Blessed Virgin for finally ridding them of her. Nonni was well loathed on both sides of the ocean, though I never learned enough of the meaty details.

THE DAY BEFORE my therapy appointment I cleaned my apartment. Months had passed since my last effort. I started in the kitchenette with the counters and sink. I cleaned the refrigerator and washed the floor. One person doesn't make much of a mess. I changed the sheets on the futon. I vacuumed the carpet, chair, and spider webs in the corners of the ceiling. I sorted things on the coffee table, threw out old mail, put recent mail in a pile. I felt that going to my first therapy session in over a month with a clean house made sense.

I played catch up. He asked about my summer. He asked about my mother. He asked about my work. He asked about how I'd been feeling in general. He asked about my anger. I told him about visiting my mother and seeing my sister and driving home from Hampton Beach in the middle of the night, and sometimes, I felt my anger but mostly kept it under control. I told him about cooking dinner at Norman's, and Charlene, and never calling her back. He asked me how it felt being out socializing with friends. I said it was okay. But I lied. They really weren't friends. Norman is my friend. His girlfriend and Charlene I only met for the first time. Uncomfortable from the start, I drank too much wine, and went off on a couple of tangents. Nonetheless she was interested, but I didn't call her. I told him I only had one gig booked. I told him I had an appointment with my psychiatrist next week. I burned through my fifty minutes, before I got around to my wondering what I'll to do the rest of my life. He began to move the way he does, to let me know we're running out of time. They say bi-polar, anxiety disorder, attention deficit, anti-social behavior, anger and

117

rage. Who knows? I wish I could find my way back to that time when I felt safe.

I remember John Kennedy had just been shot I was sitting at our kitchen table in Medford, watching the funeral procession on the old twelve-inch black-and-white that sat on the counter. The drumming went right through me. I'd never before heard death's beat. I felt weak and faint, gasping for air, feeling that I might die. I don't know where anyone else in the family was at that moment. I only recall being alone in the house.

While cleaning the apartment I found an overdue library book, and walked to the library to return it. Once I read with an eager eye, nothing special, biography and a little history. I liked books about trips to the poles, or adventures at sea. I bought books but mostly used the library. As time has passed I read less and less. When I use the library to borrow books, I bring them back largely unread. At one time I thought reading books might help make me a better person. That the more I understood about the world around me, past, present and future, the more I might understand about myself. Now I fear with every book I read, there are too many still to be read, and no matter what information or insight I have gained from reading, it cannot help me. Nor music. Nor comedy. Nor love.

Though the book was long overdue, the woman behind the counter only charged me one dollar. It's hard to be in the library and not want to check out something. I went to the movies first. I've seen all their good movies over and over again. I looked at the new section. Steve Martin's *Pink Panther 2* had been sitting there for the last four or five months. I thought that I would look at some of the literary classics. In college I had read snippets of *Walden*, *Moby Dick*, and maybe all of *Tom Sawyer*, but couldn't remember a thing. I went to the American litera- ture section and borrowed them. I knew as I walked home, by the heft of the Melville volume, I'd never get anywhere with it. I tried *Walden* first. It seemed preachy and old-fashioned. *Tom* Sawyer was a dif- ferent matter. I found it funny and dark, and read nearly half the book before falling asleep. There's a man who hated religion.

I LIED TO MY psychiatrist. He wanted to know about the nightmares. I told him there really hadn't been any nightmares. That the dreams I could remember were nostalgic, of hanging out with my friends when I was a teenager, rolling down Snow Hill Street in the North End on homemade scooters. My cousin and I constructed them out of wood, crates we salvaged at Haymarket, and roller skate wheels attached under- neath. In another dream I'm with Mary Ann Tesoro who all the guys wanted, the kind of girl who would never have anything to do with me. Tall, juggy, and destined to make it out of Medford. Last I heard she stripped at the Caravan Club on Route 1 in Saugus. In my dream we're sitting with each other in the bushes near the railroad tracks behind Hickey Park, being real close and tender.

I didn't lie to him directly. I had dreamed those things. But I failed to mention the dream that had woken me up with the shakes, one of my typical nightmare dreams, which seem to follow the plot of a thriller movie. It's not the first time a celebrity appeared in my dreams. Why Christopher Walken played the villain in this case, I don't know. In the dream I'm the only thing standing between him and my mother. We've each got weapons in our hands, and bullets too. Neither gun is loaded. We each fumble for a bullet to put in the chamber. Somehow, I slide one in first and take a quick shot that strikes his shoulder. He falls back, but recovers, and I realize that my shot is not fatal. In the moment that he begins to load his gun, I run, screaming out to my mother that I've failed her and can't protect her. That's when I woke up.

I didn't want to talk to him about it. I didn't want to dig into it, and go over every detail. We've done things like that before. Deconstructing a dream into some mathematical explanation that I can take home and somehow use to reshape my life. All the insight in the world doesn't help when I wake from a bad dream and can't get back to sleep, my mind an

incessant loop, electrical points on my body spark-
ing unchecked. He says he doesn't treat the disease
he treats the person. He's different from my psychiatrist who died suddenly from a heart attack. That
man believed in biology. It's chemical he used to say.
We're hard-wired from the beginning. How we feel
had more to do with the wiring, than experience. My
present shrink is the opposite. To him our experi-
ences have everything to do with how we feel today.
Today I didn't want to mention my recent nightmare.

Broke, I had a taste for spaghetti with tuna. I
had bread at home and it would be cheaper to make
a sandwich, but I stopped at the store and bought
some spaghetti, knowing I had a few drops of olive
oil and garlic at home. I ate two dishes and put the
rest in the fridge for tomorrow's lunch. I checked
my messages to find that the school department
had phoned, with work for tomorrow at the Roberts
School. I phoned and left a message that I would
be there. I got some clothes in order, pulled out
the futon, and settled in early reading *Tom Sawyer*.
Tomorrow I would get to see Ms. Violi.

THE MORNING was hectic. Ms. Violi had people on
phone hold, a line of students at the desk, principal
Vickerson needing her in his office, and the subs
waiting for their assignments. When she first saw me
she seemed perturbed, and I took it personally. I had

fantasized a how was your summer conversation, and her eager to see me as I she. Instead she simply said oh hi, yes Ms. Melos' class 6th grade room 334.

I found my class, or two or three of them, out back where they're supposed to meet me. Boys and girls shouted, basketballs bounced off backboards, kids kicked soccer balls, girls jump-roped, teachers tried to rein them all in. You can always tell the strictest teachers, because their classes are already in line, and a straight one. By now word already got out about a substitute and I had to get the assistant principal, who was blowing a whistle and collecting balls, to call my class for me. They pushed him to lose his temper and threaten lunch detention. They trickled in. Some defiantly bouncing right up to the line as the assistant principal called for them to relinquish balls to him.

It got no better in class. There are certain rules we're meant to uphold as substitutes. No one can put hands on anyone else and no hats indoors are two biggies. Several of the boys refused to take their hats off when I asked, and were shoving each other back and forth, more as young bucks than real threats. I told them to keep their hands off each other, but they ignored me and eventually I couldn't get them to be seated. At that point I told them to leave the room and go to the office, but they said they weren't going anywhere. I phoned the office and explained the situation. A few minutes later the assistant principal and the re-direct coordinator appeared and took me out to the hall to get the story. They went back in the class and very sternly instructed the boys to get their things and come with them. On his way out the assistant principal gave the class a short talk on the importance of acting responsibly, especially when they have a substitute. Then he apologized to me.

They kept the boys in re-direct for the rest of the day. Re-direct is where the troublesome students hang out with their friends, and avoid class. At the same time, with the most troublesome students out of the room, the teachers have a chance to do some work. After my friends were removed, the day went rather smoothly. Oh there were kids who got out of their seats, notes tossed, and even minor physical skirmishes. But they were manageable. The teachers leave a lesson plan, and I follow it the best that I can. The older the kids, the less one on one work I have. Older kids do the work or they don't. As long as they don't cause trouble, I don't care.

I made a couple of passes by the office at the end of the day, waiting until there were as few people as possible, when I returned my key. Ms. Violi smiled at me this time. You made it through your first day she said. They had me down in the first round I told her, but I recovered and went the distance. It's nice to see you. How was your summer I inquired? She told me that she'd gone to Maine for two weeks, her children and grandchildren stayed in a big house they rented on the ocean. Sounds wonderful. It was, she said, adding now back to the real world as Mr. Lockwood brought in two boys, third or fourth graders, both crying and shouting he started it, he kicked me. That interrupted the moment. How was your summer she asked as Mr. Lockwood ordered the boys to sit and made for the principal's office? Very nice, I didn't get away much, but I had the chance to relax. Then the phone rang, and then Mr. Lockwood and the principal appeared and it looked as if they needed Ms. Violi for something. I left without saying goodbye.

THERE WAS A time when I thought I understood politics and had it all figured out, who the good guys were and who the bad guys were. I'd read a few books, too few I suppose, and found a place to channel my anger. The reason I felt so bad had to have something to do with why society sucked. If I couldn't out debate the opposition, I'd simply shout them down. I knew my cause to be the right one. It's why Claire slowly ceased to include me in her life. And it's what turned her family against me. Their catch phrase for me was, boy, is that guy angry.

There's a lot to be angry about, I've always contended. Take a look around, and you don't have to look far. Stupidity is rampant, as is racism, which I believe to be underneath this hatred from certain

Christian folk towards the new president. Funny the Christians don't want to give health care to an immigrant baby. But even with regards to the new president, it's business as usual for politicians: people haven't been bailed out, only corporations, and with tidy bonuses to boot. Wars rage on. Twenty years ago I got all worked up about these things. They somehow mattered to me. Now, I don't care. In twenty or so years I won't even be around. What do I give a shit? Humans should get what they deserve.

I've heard from people with children, that having kids changes that. That somehow knowing you are leaving someone behind heightens your concern for things like the economy, justice, the environment and health care. Perhaps this is true. If so, I'll never know the feeling. I do know that my generation sold out for a retirement plan and the safety of the suburbs. Now we're supposed to feel sorry they lost their houses, or 401(k)s, while the banks and corporations are getting richer? They bought in to it, now they'll live with it. Trickle down your ass.

I try to imagine what it would be like if I had kids. I could be a grandfather. When I think of having kids, I think of having little kids, not adult kids, and changing diapers, and not sleeping from the baby crying, and being married and working with a partner: okay you change the diaper, I'll put the bottle on. Norman says that the easiest thing to do is have a kid, and there are enough stupid people in the world, and he doesn't feel that he missed anything by not having kids.

For the next couple of weeks I got called in about every other day. All jobs were at the Roberts School. When the woman who schedules subs phoned, she'd asked did I like the Roberts. She said that when they can, they like to use the same subs at the same school. It made things easier for subs, administration, and students. I'd been stealing verbal exchanges with Ms. Violi whenever I could. Unfortunately, she was always busy. Occasionally my assigned class's lunch was scheduled when she took lunch. I'd been devising a scheme. She usually brought a lunch and ate in the faculty lounge. But it being Indian summer, she'd been taking her lunch, alone, out on the bench in front of the school.

I got a couple of more responses for gigs, one in October and one in November. I also heard back from the Hong Kong Garden in Harvard Square. I was hoping for a Friday or Saturday night, but got a Thursday in December. Each season there's fewer and fewer jobs. Maybe I'm to blame. I don't put in the effort the way I used to. You've got to be out and about. Showing up at other shows, networking as they say. I had neither the energy nor the stomach for it now. I wished for something else that I could do besides substitute teaching, so that I could say, I'm a carpenter, or I'm an architect, or computer technician, and I do stand-up on the side. That wouldn't be so bad. For years when anyone asked what I did, I said with puffed chest, I'm a stand-up comedian. But how can I say that, down to one job a month at fifty-four, and I'm not making anybody laugh?

I HATE HOW people are with their pets. Why do people talk to their pets? Sparky want to go for a walk? Sparky want a biscuit? Who's the good boy? Who's the cutest dog around? And they ask! As if the dog will answer. Sure I'd love to go for a walk, as far away from you as I can get. And they talk to their pets in those silly baby voices, the way parents talk to their babies, you know the sickening tone. Come over here and eat the kibbles Mama has for you.

Dogs are worse than cats. Cats don't want to have anything to do with people. If you are visiting someone who has cats, you don't have to pet them, be nice to them, or push them off like dogs. The problem with cats is the smell. Dogs shit outside. Cats do it inside, if you visit a cat owner, you get the piss and shit smell, and the box is usually kept in the bathroom so if I need to pee I hold my nose. Visiting people with dogs is another matter. They sniff you up and down, and usually in the crotch. They jump on you, bark at you, snarl at you, drool on you. All the while the pet owner talks to them in baby talk. Sparky be a good boy now, while Sparky's riding your leg like doggy-school's out.

Most cat owners are used to the smell, so they say things like, oh we change our box regularly enough it doesn't smell. Meanwhile you're there for dinner trying not to puke from the stench. Claire and I went to China. It wasn't my first choice but Claire had always wanted to go. We visited a market where they sold live animals of all kinds, and there were cats in cages. I remember seeing this old Chinese man, peddling away on his bicycle, a cat sitting in a basket on top of the rear wheel on his way to the wok. But what's wrong with eating a cat? How do you think the chicken or cow that you ate for dinner felt? I didn't eat cat when I was in China, but I did eat dog. It was baby dog, boned out served on a sizzling platter. Tasted like duck. We didn't finish it all and took the rest in a bag that gave us a whole new take on a familiar phrase.

My Uncle Vinny always said the only good dog is a fast dog. I once dated a woman who was one of those animal rights people. Hey, I'm all for it. No animal should be abused. But I think there should be priorities. Like people first. We were at the movies one night, a movie about an abusive father who drank and beat up his wife and kids. He beat his wife so bad she died. Well, in one of the scenes, the father went crazy and made the sons tie the family dog to a cement block, and drown it in a river. Later that my night, my girlfriend couldn't stop talking about that poor dog and how horrible that scene in the movie was. Never did she mention the wife or the kids. I decided the next time I saw her I'd give her the axe. She broke up with me by phone before I had the chance. A town can burn down while the fire department rescues a kitten stuck in a piece of PVC pipe.

OVER THE NEXT couple of weeks I got calls every other day. One day I subbed for a second grade class. Lunch was the same time as Ms. Violi. I rushed the class down to the cafeteria and left them with the loony lunch ladies, pretending not to see the one who had the hots for me, waving. I ran into the teacher's lounge, grabbed a cup of coffee, and tuna sandwich in hand I made fast for the bench at the front of the school where I found her talking with a student. He must have been in some trouble, I heard her say next time I'll call your mother now go on back and finish your lunch in the office.

Beautiful day I said. Yes it is Ms. Violi responded. Do you mind some company, I asked. She said not at all. I sat down with enough distance between us. I pulled out my tuna sandwich and opened up the wrapper. Tuna, lunch of champions I said. She laughed and said with her it's ham and cheese. She asked how things had been going for me. Overall not bad, once you weed out the troublemakers in the morning. She said that the sixth grade I'd had earlier in the week is the worst class in the school. I agreed.

I asked how things were going for her so far this school year. She'd been doing it long enough now that she learned to roll with the punches she said. I asked how long she'd been doing it. Working for the city for over twenty years, at the desk of the Roberts for fifteen. You must like it. I do she responded, adding that she loved the kids. And how many do you have, I asked? Three, her youngest was a senior in high school. You must have had them young I smiled. It didn't seem like it she said, and asked whether I had children. No. I paused, continued that sometimes I regretted it. But there's nothing I can do about it now. I have a niece and a nephew I said, but didn't tell her I'd played little part in their lives, nor they in mine. Two of her kids still lived with her. The oldest daughter lived with her new husband downstairs in the first floor apartment. I learned that she owned a two-family house that she grew up in. I wanted to know what it was like living in the same house all your life. She'd never given it much thought. When she was a kid she lived on the first floor, and when she got married she moved to the second. I asked her did she go to Everett Public Schools and she said no, she was as a Saint Agnes girl, and went to high school at the Immaculate Conception.

Suddenly that confounded lunch lady appeared and said it was time for me to get my class. It seemed as if only five minutes had passed since I sat down. I had only taken two bites out of my sandwich. I excused myself, saying it was nice to talk and headed off to retrieve my class in the schoolyard. I threw my sandwich and cold coffee in a trash barrel on the way, Ms. Violi's words turning over in my head. She was a Saint Agnes girl, and went to high school at the Immaculate Conception. I should have known. Why wouldn't she be as Catholic as the next Italian-American from Everett? She probably had a statue of Saint Anthony or the Virgin in her front yard.

I brought the class back inside and spent the rest of the afternoon wasting time. I looked through the teacher's desk. One drawer was locked, but inside the others I found paper clips, a stapler, rubber bands, rulers, pencils, erasers, hand cream, a photo of a young man and a woman at some fancy celebration, a hairbrush, nail file, cough drops, stamps, a vinyl notebook with telephone numbers in it. I let the class free-draw for the last hour, as long as students were quiet and remained in their seats, I didn't care what they did. I continued to fidget around and watch the clock, counting down the minutes to when I could hand off the key. Everything had been sucked out of me.

One of the advantages of working at the Roberts School is that I can walk. On the way home I was accosted by two young male Mormons with their clean-cut grooming and white shirts, ties and those scary backpacks that you wonder might be rigged to explode. I spotted them coming blocks away. The first one said, excuse me, has anyone ever talked to you about the *Book of Mormon*? Yes they have I blurted out, has anyone ever talked to you about the *Book of Morons*? I mean look at you two, you look like your made of plastic from a mold. God appears to some fucking crazy guy in New York, and says there are gold plates buried in them hills, and you start a fucking religion? Why don't you get a life while you still can, instead of wasting away on all this shit you've been spoon-fed since birth? Why don't you get the fuck out of Everett and leave us all alone I said, turning and storming off. Then one of them asked, while still in earshot, what are you so angry about?

AND THEN IT came to me, like it was there all along and I hadn't noticed. I only had three items in my basket, a box of linguini, a can of Italian tuna, and some apples. Diane was at register six. How to sneak past and make it to the ten-items-or-less lane? As soon as I committed myself I picked up speed and looked the other way, as if I were trying to locate something and still shopping. It didn't work. She has built in sensors. In the middle of ringing a dozen eggs she said in her mono-happy-tone, I can help you right here. It was the point of no return. I could continue ahead and make a six-lane dash to ten-items- or-less, where the cashier lolled without a customer, or turn and get in line for Diane.

I've used the same market since I moved to Everett. Diane's won more Employee of the Month awards than anyone in the history of the Mighty Mart. Diane, who always has a smile on her face, a deceptive smile, it's hard to tell if there's something wrong with her, or she's playing a joke on you. Diane, who names and counts out the produce numbers as she weighs and punches them in: broccoli seven four four one six three, apples three three two six one four, garlic one seven three nine six six, and she knows all the numbers and never stops to look like the other cashiers. And she tells you your total and how much you saved with your preferred shoppers card. And your total today is $13.27. And today with your preferred shoppers card you saved $1.21. Now will that be debit or credit today? If you use your debit card you may take cash back.

Diane, who bags obsessively and warns, here is your bread bag so it doesn't get squished, careful with those eggs I put them on top for you. Diane, who never strays from task, no talk of the Red Sox or recent rain. I can help you right here she nails another trying to sneak past her three-carriage backup, while other cashiers stand around doing nothing.

I can help you right here. Why not? Why would anyone who featured at Milky's open mic in Leominster, have any shame about such a catch phrase? I could be a fifty-four year old male cashier. Is he stupid, or laughing at the world? Always a smile, knows every PLU number, able to take on three times the volume of lesser cashiers. Who never flinches under pressure, never a bead of sweat! Whose bagging prowess is heralded throughout the nine store region, and beyond to other market chains! At one time Foodbasket made a play for him but he declined. I can help you right here. His call to arms. Stop where you are. Go no further. You are safe with me. I do everything right. I have never called in sick. Am never seen without my smile. Everything is great. I can help you right here. Did you find everything you need? If you plan on using your debit card you may get cash back. That's corn two seven four five five nine and pears three three six four eight seven and would you like paper or plastic? I doubled up the bags on your canned goods and you saved $4.32 with you preferred customer card today. You have yourself a good day now. I can help you right here.

I'd have to find the right voice. There'd be more real acting in this bit. And how could I work it into my show, without cutting a lot of the material I'd been polishing for years? But maybe it was time. Maybe I had a few more laughs up my sleeve. I refused sub work the next morning. The woman who calls me seemed surprised. I knew that saying no meant running the risk of getting bumped down a couple of names on the list. I didn't care. Anxious to get right to work on my now Fifty-Four-Year-Old

Male Mighty Mart Cashier, I decided to take the day and do some real work. Besides, I wanted to put some distance between Ms. Violi and me. I couldn't rid myself of the memory of how she beamed when she said I'm a Saint Agnes girl. Immaculate Conception my ass.

At the café I drank three espressos and brainstormed for a couple of hours. I filled dozens of pages in my notebook. It wasn't my style, to write in a café, but I needed to get out of the apartment. The girl next door had thrown up in the morning, and it reminded me that the guy next door had thrown up last night, the apartment felt especially small. Eventually I returned home, my system racing from the espressos, and began working on a voice. I did bits and pieces of things, and listened back on my tape recorder. When I struck the right tone and cadence I'd know it. High, low, fast, slow, I tried as many variations as I could. Finally I got it. I'd been trying to imitate Diane, her timbre. Suddenly, fifty or sixty tries later I heard it. It was my own.

For several hours into the evening I worked in front of the bathroom mirror. I tried hundreds of different smiles. The smile would be everything, because it could not change once I went into the bit. When I felt I had the smile, I began to improv. I did whatever came into my head, and experimented with every conceivable imagining of Fifty-Four Year Old Male Mighty Mart Cashier.

The good thing about the character is that I could change the age every year I got older. I could eventually be the Seventy-Five Year Old Male Mighty Mart Cashier. I tried numerous variations, and imagined skit after skit. I worked up a bit where I ring up my one-millionth customer. The local press is there to witness as I put my finger to the register's total button. In another I'm training new cashiers—the vapid high school boy who stares off when I tell him something, the first-job-after-six-kids housewife, the neurotic teenaged girl who begins every sentence asking know what? In still another I am awarded a cashier's lifetime achievement award. And then there's the new upstart cashier trying to move in on my territory. I can help you right here. There were so many possibilities. I fantasized a supermarket sit-com. I can help you riiiiggghhht here. I'd be a talk show guest. Paparazzi would take my photo coming out of restaurants. It could be the latest phrase around the coffee machine circuit. I can help you RRRIIIIIIIIGGHHHHT here! Let me dream if I want to. I looked at the clock and realized I'd been going for twelve hours. I warmed up the leftover spaghetti with tuna from the night before. I ate like a man who'd been working the fields all day.